EUSTACIA GOES TO THE
CHALET SCHOOL

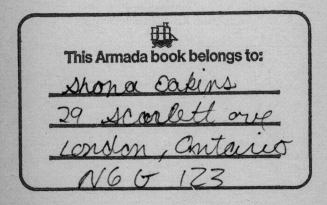

First published in the U.K. in 1929 by
W. & R. Chambers Ltd., London and Edinburgh.
This edition was first published in Armada in 1969 by
Fontana Paperbacks,
14 St. James's Place, London SW1A 1PS.

This impression 1982.

© W. & R. Chambers Ltd. 1929.

Printed in Great Britain by
Love & Malcomson Ltd.,
Brighton Road, Redhill, Surrey.

EUSTACIA GOES TO THE TO THE CHALET SCHOOL

Elinor M. Brent-Dyer

Armada

CONTENTS

Chapter 1

EUSTACIA

THERE is no disguising the fact that Eustacia Benson was the most arrant little prig that ever existed. Her father, a learned professor of Greek, and mother, a doctor, both had great theories on how to bring up children, and to these they subjected their only child, the unfortunate Eustacia—so called because of the meaning of the name in Greek, 'rich in corn', which the professor interpreted as 'rich in knowledge'. We have little difficulty in guessing the effect of those theories when we meet Eustacia for the first time one day in November, sitting in the drawing-room at her Aunt Margery's, looking round it with a superior air, and mentally deciding how *she* would re-arrange the room, should it be given over to her.

In the preceding June, Mrs. Benson died of pneumonia. Eustacia had mourned properly. Then she had settled down to play mistress in the big house; and her father, immersed in his classics, had let her go her own way. Three weeks before this story opens, he had had a violent attack of pain, which had sent him to a doctor, who sounded him, asked him sundry questions, and then told him gently that he had come too late. He was in the last stages of heart disease.

There was little the doctor could do. He impressed on the dying man, however, that he ought to let his relations know, and the professor actually managed to remember and wrote a brief note to his wife's only sister.

Mrs. Trevanion promptly came to Oxford, and stayed there till the end came, as it did five days later. The housemaid, going into the study one morning to attend to her work, found the professor sitting at his desk, his head down on the papers lying there. She had flown for Mrs. Trevanion, and then to the telephone for the doctor. There was nothing to be done, however. He had been dead some hours, and it was obvious that death had come painlessly.

There was, then, only Eustacia to settle, and her fate was settled for her, for when the professor's will was opened they found that he had appointed her Aunt Margery as her guardian; her uncle, Edmund Trevanion, as her trustee; and she was to be sent to school at once. This was something of a relief to Mrs. Trevanion, who, during the short time she had been there, had found herself utterly confounded by her unchildlike niece, who frequently put her right on matters with an aplomb that would have been irritating had it not been funny.

The Trevanions had five boys—the eldest fifteen, and the youngest three. Eustacia was almost fourteen, and Mrs. Trevanion well knew that the very self-sufficient young person in the grey frock, with long hair worn in two tight pigtails, would have anything but an easy time of it with them. However, she wanted to get back to her home and family, and she could scarcely leave the child alone in Oxford, so she told her gently that they must pack. The great house would be closed for a while, till she and Mr. Trevanion could see their way clear to arranging matters, and Eustacia was to go back to Devonshire with them.

Eustacia had disputed this at first, arguing that she could quite well stay where she was. She had been mistress in the house since her mother's death, and could go on till it was time for her to go to school. She hated the idea of school and endless silly girls who were empty-headed and frivolous. Still, as her father had insisted on it in his will, she supposed she must go. But she could stay in Oxford till then, thank you.

Mrs. Trevanion, who had been condescendingly corrected more than once that morning, was impatient, and showed it. 'Nonsense!' she said.

'But it is not nonsense, my dear aunt,' said Eustacia. 'It is quite sensible. I have no desire to leave Oxford, and I can manage the house and servants quite well.'

A battle ensued, in which Mrs. Trevanion won, as might have been supposed, and on the day named, three people arrived in Taverton in South Devon late that night. Two were tired and cross, and one was sulky. The boys had all gone to bed before their parents and cousin reached home, and the meeting with Eustacia was staved off till next morning. Then they met, and it did not take any of the young Trevanions—from Ned, the eldest, to Baby Frank—long to

6

decide that they had never met such a disagreeable girl in their lives. Worse than all, she told tales to her aunt and uncle. When Humphrey made her an apple-pie bed, she marched downstairs to the drawing-room and dragged her aunt up to see it, instead of taking it as a joke. Ned, roused to fury by her criticisms, pulled one of her long plaits, and she promptly rushed away to her uncle's 'den', to tell him of the outrage. Ned got a thrashing for 'bullying', and Eustacia a lecture on 'sneaking' which astonished her.

On the morning of that very day, Mrs. Trevanion, calling her sons together, had implored them not to tease their cousin. 'She doesn't understand,' she said. 'She doesn't know how wrong it is to tell tales. Do be dear boys while she is with us, and let her alone. Remember how short a time it is since she lost her father and mother, and make allowances for her.'

The boys promised to do their best, but they all agreed with Gill when he said imploringly, 'Oh, Mums! can't you send her to a school where they don't *have* holidays?'

It is true Mrs. Trevanion agreed with his spirit, but she rebuked him for unkindness to his cousin. Secretly, she too would have been glad to hear of just such a school, for, during the short time she had been in Taverton, Eustacia had contrived to set everyone by the ears.

'The house isn't the same, Mun,' she said despairingly to her husband. 'And now, Julia has given notice. She says that she won't put up with the way Miss Eustacia orders her about. And she is such a nice girl—so pleasant in her ways, and so fond of the boys. It's too bad!'

He laughed; advised her to tell Julia that Eustacia would not be staying there after Christmas, and went off to business. His wife, with a resigned face, put on her things and went out to do the shopping. In the greengrocer's she met with an acquaintance, a Mrs. Cochrane, step-mother of the Grizel Cochrane of other chronicles of the Chalet School, and to her she unburdened herself.

'What an objectionable child she seems!' said Mrs. Cochrane. 'Well, Grizel has always been a nuisance, but, thank goodness, she was never as bad as that! And that reminds me, Mrs. Trevanion, I believe I can solve your problem for you. Send your niece to the Chalet School. I can recommend it unreservedly. Grizel had four years there, you know, and she is very much improved. It belongs to

Madge Bettany—do you remember them? They lived in Greenacres, that house the Corah Mine people took for their managers. Madge went out to Austria to start a school after the death of their guardian, and it has been highly successful. Of course, she is married now, and, I believe, has only a financial interest in it; but I know it is still flourishing. And it has this great advantage. It is so far away that it would scarcely be worth while for the child to come home for any holidays save the summer one. If any school could do your niece good, I feel sure the Chalet would. Two terms there might make a different girl of her. I advise you to write to Mademoiselle, the present Head, at once. Walk round with me, and I'll give you the prospectus now. I can show you some of Grizel's letters too, and you will see by them how happy the girls are. It would take her right away from her old surroundings too, and that ought to help matters.'

Mrs. Trevanion liked the idea. She had known Madge Bettany quite well, and also Mademoiselle Lepâttre. The prospectus, with its delightful photographs, was most alluring; and Grizel's letters showed what a good time the girls had and how they loved their school. Surely this was the very thing for Eustacia. And she might have a better chance among foreigners, who would be more likely to make allowances for the girl's unfortunate ways than English girls. The more she thought of it, the more she fell in love with the idea. Finally she went off to finish her shopping, taking the prospectus and some of Grizel's letters with her to show her husband; and that night, when the children were all in bed, they talked the matter over, and finally decided that, if the Heads of the Chalet School would take her, Eustacia should go there at the beginning of the next term. The mere mixing with other girls ought to be good for her, and they hoped that the summer holidays would bring back to England a different Eustacia.

Accordingly, Mrs. Trevanion wrote to Mademoiselle Lepâttre, explaining matters clearly, and then awaited results. She also wrote to Madge Bettany, now Madge Russell. She received replies that both Mademoiselle and Mrs. Russell were willing to have Eustacia at the Chalet School. The Easter term began in the third week in January, as one of the old girls was to be married then, and the entire school had been invited to be present at the function. As

Eustacia and the two or three other new girls would have no interest in it, Mademoiselle suggested that they should not come until the Friday—the wedding would take place on the Wednesday. Thus she would fall right into school life at once. A new mistress, who was joining the staff, would meet her in London on the Wednesday, and would act as escort to the Tiernsee.

'Boarding-school!' cried Eustacia, when she had heard. 'You are sending me to boarding-school? But why? I wish to attend the High School here. I must have some home-life. It is that which helps to form character.'

Her aunt shook her head. 'I cannot keep you here, Eustacia. You have upset the whole house in the short time we have had you. You have never once tried to think of anyone but yourself. You have told tales, been rude to the maids, behaved in a most unfitting way to both your uncle and myself, and are making the boys unhappy.'

'If your sons tease and torment me, it is only right you should know of it,' said Eustacia priggishly. 'As for the servants, they are only servants, and are here to do as they are told. And you think of your boys' unhappiness, Aunt Margery, but never trouble about mine. I am an orphan. I have only you to whom to look for affection—and you show yours by driving me away from the house and sending me to a school in a place with an outlandish name, where I shall be with complete strangers.'

'That is true,' said Mrs. Trevanion quietly. 'But, Eustacia, will you ask yourself in *what* ways you have tried to show yourself lovable since you came here? You have never once thought of anyone but yourself. You have repelled any show of affection, and you have made the whole house miserable. We are sending you to school that you may learn the art of living with other people. When we meet in the summer I hope you will understand all this, and show yourself so pleasant, so jolly, so fair that we shall be glad to have you back, and sorry to lose you once more. But that will depend on yourself entirely.'

Eustacia stood, strangely silent for her. She was hurt that she, Eustacia Benson, who was always right, should be so lectured. But she had a strain of honesty in her that made her own to herself, at any rate, that her aunt was right. She had *not* been 'lovable'. But the strain of honesty was over-laid by a thick veneer of foolish training, and she turned

9

away, saying, 'I am not demonstrative by nature, Aunt Margery, but I cannot help thinking your behaviour to your orphan niece most unkind and unnatural.'

Mrs. Trevanion let her go. There was nothing to be done for her as yet. Only time and experience and rubbing shoulders with other people could help her to become what, at present, she was not; and to those three things the lady wisely resolved to leave her.

Chapter II

'WHAT AN AWFUL NAME!'

'LETTERS, Madge!' Joey Bettany came rushing into the big salon at Die Rosen, where her elder sister was sitting sewing while her small son rolled on his crawling-rug at her feet.

Madge Russell, still as youthful in appearance as when she had first come out to the Tyrol to open the Chalet School, four years before, dropped her work and took the handful of letters Joey held out to her. 'Here you are, Jo,' she said, giving the girl two thick packages. 'These are for Jem—run and put them on the table in his study, will you? And then call up to Mademoiselle. There are a good many here for her.'

'Righto! I'll be back anon,' said Jo.

Madge glanced across at her son to be sure that he was all right, and then opened the first of the batch that had come for her. She was deep in it when kind, plain-faced Mademoiselle Lepâttre, active partner in the Chalet School, came quietly into the room, to seek her letters and sit down on the other side of the great porcelain stove. During the winter the postman only found his way up to the Sonnalpe twice in the week, and he generally brought a heavy mail with him. Dr. Jem, head of the great sanatorium there, was always inundated with correspondence; his wife had many letters from friends and old girls; and the many invalids usually received one or two at the very least, so Herr Sneider was wont to bemoan the weight of the mail-

10

bags he bore on his back on those days when he climbed up the mountain-path. However, he always found a good meal awaiting him in the kitchen of Marie and Andreas, the two servants at Die Rosen, and, as he had to wait for replies, he had a long rest.

Joey Bettany fulfilled her commission of delivering Dr. Jem's letters and returned to the salon, accompanied by the Robin, whose father was secretary to the sanatorium. The two school-girls entered quietly, and Joey flopped down on the crawling-rug beside her nephew, while the Rob ran to 'Tante Marguérite', who had come to take the place of her dead mother in her heart, and scrubbed her black curls well into the lap of the gentle woman, who dropped her letter and picked her up.

'What is it, Robinette?' asked Madge Russell, with a suspicion that all was not well.

'Been—naughty,' murmured the small maid confusedly.

'What have you been doing?' asked Madge resignedly.

'*Only* frowed water out of the window and hit Eigen,' said the Robin, her black lashes sweeping scarlet cheeks as she confessed her crime.

Mademoiselle looked up with a gentle, 'But, Robin, that was not *gentille*!'

'Why did you do that, *mein Blümchen*?' asked Mrs. Russell.

' 'Cos I wanted to empty the basin.'

'Isn't there a bathroom in the house?' questioned Madge gravely.

'Ye-es; but it was so far.'

Madge shook her head. 'Not too far; not really far at all. You were lazy, Robin. Now, I forbid you to do that again. And you must apologise to Eigen for wetting him. I shall ring the bell and ask Marie to send him here.'

Madge Russell had once said that there were only two really effective punishments for the Robin, for she was so delicate that many measures of discipline had to be neglected in her case. But to see her beloved Jo in trouble through her fault, or to be made to apologise for any of her small misdeeds, were quite enough for her. Once, and once only, had the child tried to coax her father into letting her forgo the latter. He had listened to her, and then had asked gently, 'Does Tante Marguérite say you must, my darling?'

'She said so,' acknowledged the Robin unwillingly.

'Then I'm afraid you *must*, little daughter. Tante Marguérite loves you too well ever to order you to do anything really hurtful to you. You must be obedient, my pet; and you must not be naughty. Never again ask me to change a punishment of hers, for I shall not do it.'

It was a sharp lesson, gently spoken as the words were; but the Robin never forgot it. Now, she scrambled off Mrs. Russell's knee, and rang the bell herself, though her baby soul was outraged at the thought of what must follow. Mademoiselle, with understanding, got up and left the room, and Joey ran after her. So there was only 'Tante Marguérite' to witness the entrance of Eigen, still damp from his unexpected shower-bath, and the Robin's faltered apology. Eigen took it uncomfortably, but Madge would not let the small girl off, despite his imploring eyes. It was gone through, and he was dismissed, to get hot coffee from his sister Marie, who ruled in the kitchen, after he had changed his coat. Then there was a little tender loving talk on the naughtiness of throwing water out of windows, and the wrong of pride that hated to say, 'I'm sorry'.

'You are a little girl,' said Madge. 'A little girl may do many wrong and foolish things, and when they offend other people, then they must be apologised for.'

What else she might have had to say on the subject will never be known, for at that moment Joey came tumbling into the room, to announce, 'Mademoiselle says there's *another* new pupil for the School. She's got a letter—coming to tell you all about it!'

'Joey! I wish you wouldn't burst into rooms as abruptly as you do,' said Madge severely.

'Sorry,' apologised Jo.

'I should think so. Please don't do it again. You are quite old enough to be more grown-up now. Sixteen—and you often behave like six!'

Jo's face fell. 'Well, I *am* sorry,' she murmured uncertainly.

Happily, however, Mademoiselle came in, an open letter in her hand and her kind face beaming with excitement. 'Listen, *chérie*! We are offered a new pupil for the School —and from Taverton, too!'

'From Taverton?' Madge's interest was promptly aroused. 'Who can it be?'

'Do you remember Mrs. Trevanion?' asked Mademoiselle.

'Yes; of course I do! A pretty little woman, with a swarm of small boys. Surely she isn't proposing to send any of them *here*?' laughed Madge.

'It is not her sons, but a niece she wishes to send,' said Mademoiselle—they were all speaking in French at the moment. 'It seems that this child is peculiar. But I will read to you what she says.'

She cleared her throat, and read aloud: ' "The fact of the matter is, my dear Mademoiselle, my niece has been far too long with elderly people—there were twenty years between my sister and myself—and she needs companions of her own age. She talks and behaves on most occasions like an elderly lady, and I do not think it healthy. On thinking matters over, it struck both my husband and myself that it would be far better for Eustacia to begin in a school such as yours. I doubt very much if she would be happy with the average English girl. French and Austrian girls, brought up, as I am aware, to far less freedom than those of our own country, might notice all this less, and so make it easier for her to settle down. As soon as Mrs. Cochrane told me of the school, and showed me some of Grizel's old letters, I felt it was the solution to our problem. I do so hope and trust you and Mrs. Russell will be able to take her".'

'The rest of the letter relates to business,' went on Mademoiselle, folding it up. 'That is all that need concern us at the moment. What do you think, Marguérite?'

'It's the most sensible thing they could have done,' said Madge briskly. 'She is quite right in what she says. Such a girl would be most unhappy at first in a High School, and might make things very difficult for herself. Here, where the girls are all trained to much more precise manners from their very babyhood, it will not make so much difference. Take her by all means, if you can fit her in.'

Mademoiselle thought for a moment or two. 'We can manage, I think,' she said. 'We are now eighty in number, and I do not wish to crowd the girls more than is already done. But there is that little room at Le Petit Chalet, where two beds might be put. Then two more of the younger middles could sleep there, and that would leave us two beds for this Eustacia Benson and the little one from Russia.

13

But, unless we build, Marguérite, we can take only a certain number at midsummer, and none for next term, unless any should leave us at the end of this.'

'Mary *is* leaving,' put in Joey, with a sigh for the head-girl, who was a good friend of hers.

'But she is only one,' said Mademoiselle.

'We may take one new girl for the summer term, but that will be all.'

'Maynie's leaving too,' went on Jo. 'I wish people wouldn't get married!'

'Now, Jo,' said Madge. 'Maynie has had to put off her wedding once already, and we've had her four years. In another year Juliet will be with us to take her place, and we must just manage till then.'

'But *I* shan't be here then,' protested the pessimist. 'Oh, I *hate* changes!'

'Still, my child, they have to be,' Mademoiselle reminded her. 'We should not progress else.'

Jo wriggled her shoulders. 'I know that. But it doesn't make me like them any better. Now Bernhilda's going to be married soon; and then I'm sure Bette is almost betrothed. She blushed like anything when we met her and Frau Rincini and that youth in the Maria-Theresien café on Christmas Eve.'

'Yes; I expect Bette will be betrothed shortly,' agreed Madge. 'Still, if it makes them happy, Jo——'

Jo scowled. 'They might wait a little, I think.'

Madge laughed. 'Girls grow up very quickly out here, Joey. Never mind! You and Juliet and my Robin shall stay little girls as long as you like!'

'But Juliet will be quite grown up when she teaches us,' said the Robin seriously. 'And, please, what is the name of the new girl?'

'Eustacia Benson,' said Madge.

'Coo! What a name!' said Jo. 'What an *awful* name! It's enough to make her weird!'

'I do not like it,' said the Robin thoughtfully.

'Perhaps she will permit that we call her "Stacie",' suggested Mademoiselle.

'That would be better,' acknowledged Jo. 'All the same, it *is* an awful name, and you can *not* say that it isn't.'

The entry of Dr. Jem at this point caused them to shelve the subject; but Jo had by no means forgotten it, and when

Madge went, as was her custom, to say good-night after her sister had gone to bed, she found a wide-awake Jo, whose last words to her were 'Good-night! Sleep well! Eustacia! It's enough to scare the birds!'

Chapter III

BERNHILDA'S WEDDING

IT was all settled. Eustacia was to come to the Chalet School on the Friday of the week term began. After that, they hoped she would settle down quickly and be very happy with them. A long letter from Mrs. Trevanion to Madge had amplified what the first had told them, and that young lady had had a long serious talk with Mademoiselle. There could be no doubt of it—they were undertaking a difficult task.

'Still,' said the young owner of the school, 'I expect she'll shake down pretty quickly, once she gets accustomed to being with other girls.'

'I trust so, *chérie*,' said Mademoiselle.

After that, no one thought very much about school, for everyone was far too busy with the wedding of Bernhilda Mensch, one of the first girls to attend the school, to trouble about outside affairs.

It was by no means the first wedding among the old girls of the Chalet School. The previous year had seen the wedding of Gisela Marani and Bernhilda's brother, Gottfried. In the summer, Wanda von Eschenau, the loveliest girl the school had ever had, had married a young captain in the Austrian army, one Friedel von Glück. But Bernhilda and her *Bräutigam*, Kurt von Eschenau, were leaving Austria altogether for France, where Kurt had a post in a big shipping merchant's, and they would not see her very frequently. Gisela lived at the Sonnalpe, where Gottfried was one of the assistant doctors at the great sanatorium, and Wanda was in Vienna. But Bernhilda, in Lyons, would be far away. Therefore, the girls who loved her felt that they must make much of her, and give her happy days to remember when she should have left them.

The girls came to school on the Monday, and early on Tuesday afternoon they all set off down the snow-covered mountain-path leading to Spärtz, the little town on the Innsbruck-Wien line at the foot of the mountains, to take the train for Innsbruck, where the Mensches lived. The staff and the Russells accompanied them, but Gisela was left at home, though her young husband would walk down early the next morning to attend the marriage of his pretty sister. Bernhilda came to the Sonnalpe at the week-end, to say 'good-bye' to her sister-in-law, and went down on the Monday with her father, known to Joey and the Robin as 'Onkel Reise', because of his great size, to spend the last two days of her maidenhood at home, where her mother moved about chattering gaily, and her father sat looking at her with loving eyes, and the very old *Grossmutter*, who had reached her century a few weeks before, gave her good advice.

On the Tuesday, when all the unpacking had been done and everything was ready for work, the girls sat down to a hurried meal at twelve o'clock, and then, with festal garments in light wicker baskets—one basket to five girls—they wrapped up warmly, and set off on their long tramp.

It was dusk when they reached the little town, where lights twinkled from the windows, and the *Bahnhof* sent forth a stream of yellow glowing over the white snow. The Robin and sundry others of the juniors were almost asleep by the time the city was reached, and had to be roused to get them out; but once they had left the *Bahnhof* and were out in the Bahnhof Platz, the cold air woke them up effectually, and they crowded round their mistresses, chattering eagerly. Many of the girls had homes in Innsbruck, and these were claimed by parents who had come for the purpose, and were whirled off, always with one or two additions from those who lived at a distance. The Russells, Joey, and the Robin went off with the Maranis as soon as Madge had seen the last of the School marching across to the 'Europa', where rooms had been taken for all who could not be accommodated by the friendly Tyroleans, and were soon running up the stairs of a tall house where the Maranis had a flat on the fourth *étage*.

On the way home, Maria had aroused all Joey's curiosity by saying that there was a great surprise for them at home, and the pair simply tore up the stairs, arriving hot and breathless at the landing.

'Come,' said Maria, as she rang the doorbell. A pretty maid, in the picturesque garb of Tyrolean servants, opened to them, and Maria ran in, followed by Jo. They passed the door of the *Speisesaal*, and went on to the salon. There the small Austrian threw open the door and stood back for her friend to enter. Jo walked in, looking round eagerly for the promised surprise. It came from a low chair beside the stove, in the shape of a tall, fair girl with very dark eyes, who rose to her feet and held out her arms, with a little cry—'Joey!'

'Juliet!' Jo rushed to her and hugged her vehemently. 'Oh, Juliet! What a *gorgeous* surprise! When did you come? Did Frau Marani ask for you specially? How have you managed about coll? How long are you going to stay? Oh, isn't this *golloptious*?'

Before Juliet could answer any of the string of questions, steps sounded outside, and the Robin came running in. Then the Russells followed, Madge almost as excited as the two children, and Dr. Jem very pleased, for neither had known of this surprise planned by kind Herr Marani and his pretty wife. Juliet had left the Chalet School eighteen months before to go to the Royal Holloway College to read for her degree in mathematics, and none of them had seen her since. It had been intended that she should return for the long vacation in the previous summer; but she had managed to catch scarlet-fever just before it began, and by the time she was well again there was only a fortnight left to her, and Madge and Jem had written to say that she had far better not risk the long tiring journey so soon after her sharp illness. She had, accordingly, spent the fortnight with young Mrs. Cowley, who, hearing from Madge of the happening, had promptly written off to the girl to demand that she should be the first visitor in the pretty new home. Juliet had been glad to accept, for she was very homesick, and not strong after the fever. The attack had been a bad one, and even the fortnight on the south coast had not been sufficient to brace her properly, as she now explained to the assembled crowd. She had suffered from bad headaches during the term, and had found it difficult to get on with her work. The doctor, therefore, had advised a holiday for a few weeks, and when Frau Marani's invitation to her for

Bernhilda's wedding had come, she had written to accept at once, knowing that when the great event was over she could go up to the Sonnalpe with the Russells, and stay there till she was all right again.

'Then you *must* come to School, if it's only for a few days!' declared Joey.

Juliet laughed. 'What do *you* think, Jo? Of course I'm coming. Besides, I want to go to the Sonnalpe and see Gisela. Hard luck she couldn't get down for Bernie's wedding!'

'Gisela is very busy, and quite happy to stay where she is,' said Madge, with a smile. 'And now, come and be introduced to my son, Juliet. There! What do you think of him?' She took him from Frau Marani, who had been holding him all this time, and put him into Juliet's arms.

Juliet kissed him, and then gave him back to his mother. 'He's a lovely baby, Madame. Just exactly like you—though I think he has a look of Dr. Jem too. How old is he now?'

'Nine months,' said Madge, as she hushed the baby in her arms. 'It's no use, I'm afraid. He wants bed, and nothing else will serve him—Frau Marani, if you will forgive me, I think I'll just undress him and pop him in at once. He's too tired to be good tonight!'

Frau Marani nodded understandingly. 'But of course, *mein Liebling*. Come to your room.—And, Maria, bring the warm water for the bath. Anna has it ready, I am sure.'

This broke up the circle, and while Maria ran to the *Küche* for the bath-water, Mrs. Russell went off with her son, and Juliet led Joey and the Robin to the pretty room they three were to share. There, while the two younger girls changed, she sat on the foot of her bed and talked eagerly with them, asking questions about everyone she had known, and hearing about those she had not. When they were ready, they went into the salon again, and there Juliet was plied with questions about college till the elders came back.

Baby David was now safely in his cot and sleeping peacefully, and Mrs. Russell had changed her frock too. 'We are longing for you to come back to us,' she said, as she sat down beside the tall, slim girl. 'Has Jo told you that we are losing Miss Maynard at the end of this half-term?'

Juliet nodded. 'I know. Oh, Madame, I shall love to come back; but with you and Maynie and Miss Durrant gone, to say nothing of all the girls who were there with

18

me, it won't be the same thing. Jo says Rosalie has left, and Mary is leaving. And she will be the next to go, I suppose?'

Mrs. Russell looked across at her husband with a smile. 'Shall we tell them, Jem?'

'Might as well,' he said lazily.

"Well, then, Jo is staying till next mid-summer. After many consultations, we all agreed that it would be better for her not to take up her duties as lady-in-waiting to Elisaveta till she was eighteen. So we are to keep her with us till then.'

Silence greeted her remarks. Then Joey jumped up from her seat. 'Madge! Do you mean it? Am I really to have a year more than I thought at school? Oh! How—how *great*! It isn't that I don't like Elisaveta,' said Jo soberly. 'I *do*. She's a dear. And so is King Carol. Only, being a lady-in-waiting seems so grown up. I'll have a topping time for my last year, anyway!'

Madge looked serious. 'That depends on what you call "a topping time", Joey. You see, we have decided that you are to be head-girl when Mary goes.'

Joey stood stock-still in the shock of the announcement. 'D'you *mean* it?' she gasped, when she had recovered her breath.

'Yes,' said her sister.

Joey sat down. 'How—how simply sickening!" she said fervently.

'*Joey!*' Madge sounded properly shocked.

'Well, it *is*! I'll have to behave like an angel without wings, and there isn't much fun in *that*! Oh, Madge, need I? Can't you choose someone else?'

Madge shook her head. 'No, Joey. It is all settled, and you are to be head-girl. After all, it isn't much to ask in return for all the fun you've had. You are growing up now —yes, you are, whether you like it or not—and it is only right that you should take some of the responsibilities of the School on your shoulders. But now, we have been talking "shop" rather rudely.—Frau Marani, please forgive us.'

Frau Marani, a pretty woman of nearly forty, nodded, and laughed. 'But we have all been much interested.— Have we not, Florian?' She turned to her husband.

He agreed. 'It is all of great interest to us—our dear Chalet School. I am sure that Jo will do her best to keep

19

it to the high standard that you, *liebe Dame*, have instituted.—It is an honour, Joey, *mein Kind*.'

'It's one I could very well do without,' grumbled Joe. 'Oh, all right! If you say I've got to take it on, I suppose I've got to. But I think it's hard lines for all that!'

At this point the Robin created a diversion by falling off the chair in which she had been sleepily nodding for the last twenty minutes, and Frau Marani rose and decreed that she should go to bed at once. Half an hour later, the two younger girls were despatched bedwards, for, as their gentle hostess observed, there would be plenty for them to do on the morrow and it was already eight o'clock, and Jo, at least, was tired after the long walk down from the Tiernsee. They went, Jo because she was tired out, and Maria because she had been brought up to be instantly and cheerfully obedient to the lightest word of either father or mother.

Once the 'children' had gone, the elders drew their chairs closer and had a long chat about school, Gisela Mensch, Bernhilda, and the thousand and one things that interested them all. The Robin formed one of the subjects of the conversation.

'Yes; she is stronger,' said the doctor, in answer to a query from Herr Marani. 'Fortunately she has missed the chicken-pox epidemic we had a few weeks ago, and her general health is improving. We must watch her closely for the next few years, but I believe that if we can get her safely past the growing years, all fear of tuberculosis will be at an end, humanly speaking. Luckily, her own happy nature is a big asset, and she has been taught obedience from the very first, so we have no frettings and grumblings over her limitations, as we might have had from an English or American child.'

'Treason!' cried Madge, laughing. 'Why, pray, should you run down the children of your own country?'

'My dear girl,' he said seriously, 'you know as well as I do that the majority of English and American children are nowadays allowed to "develop their own personalities", which, in nine cases out of ten, means that they are allowed to do pretty much as they like. Now, the Robin has never known that. She has always understood that when she was told to do a thing it must be done without grumbling or fretting, and the good results are being shown in the way

20

her strength is growing. I can assure you, I intend to see that David grows up to render absolute obedience to both of us.'

'I think you are right,' said Herr Marani, as Madge remained silent. 'The obedient child is the happy child. Although, I think that there are many of our compatriots who do not insist on it as they should. I should be sorry, for instance, to have Maria behave as her little cousins, Sophie and Anita Rincini, too often do. But that is the fault of the parents.'

Juliet sat thoughtfully turning all this over in her mind. 'I think you are right, Onkel Florian,' she said suddenly. 'If I had learnt to do as I was told when I was small, I might have been all right by this time, instead of feeling horrid as I do. You see,' she went on with an effort, 'I ought to have taken a longer vac after fever, but I wouldn't listen to anyone, and insisted on going back to coll. Now I've got to pay up for it.'

'I'll examine you tomorrow, Julie,' promised the doctor. 'And now we've got you here, we mean to take good care of you, and see to it that you don't go back to work till you are quite fit.'

'And now it is time we all retired,' said Frau Marani, rising. 'Hark! That is twenty-three o'clock, and we shall have much excitement tomorrow. So, let us say *Gute Nacht*, and seek our pillows.'

Chapter IV

THE WEDDING

THE next morning all was bustle and excitement. The wedding would take place in the church of St. Nicholas, at midday. The Maranis lived near Wilten, some distance from the Mariahilfe, where was the home of the Mensches, and it meant leaving early. By ten o'clock they were all ready. Joey, Maria, and the Robin were in their white frocks, and the two latter had their hair tied with white ribbons. They all wore cloaks over their dresses, and hoods to match, and, of course, they went by sleigh, for the streets were deep in frozen snow and wheels would not have been safe.

They drove to the tall house in the Mariahilfe, where they saw the bride, very fair and sweet in her plain satin gown, her veil of white net and lace fastened by the wreath of myrtle all Tyrolean brides wear. Madge and Frau Marani kissed her, and then went on to the church with Juliet, while Joey, Maria, and Robin waited with Maria von Eschenau, prettier than ever in her white frock; for they four, together with Bernhilda's younger sister, Frieda, were to be the bridesmaids to the bride. They went into the salon to make their curtseys to *die Grossmutter*, who sat in her chair, very frail and small, but with her indomitable spirit glowing in her black eyes, and she made them turn round, and then commented on their attire. Jo was sent off to brush her unruly locks again, and Maria to pull her stockings straighter; but the Robin was only kissed and crooned over. Nearly seventy years before, old Frau Mensch had lost a little daughter, who had had the same rosy cheeks, black curls, and deep brown eyes as the small maid, and though most had forgotten the bare existence of Baby Natalie, her mother still cradled her in her heart, and the Robin had crept very near to that sacred spot.

When they were ready they got into the sleigh, and so reached the church, where their cloaks were taken from them by an attendant, and they were ushered into a back seat to await the coming of the bride. She came at length, her face pale with emotion under her long veil, and they formed up behind her, and the white-clad procession drifted up the aisle to wonderful music from the organ-loft; for Bernhilda's uncle was a bishop, and had come to perform the ceremony, and Kurt's cousin was a Benedictine monk who was famed for his music, and had come to play for the bridal of his young cousin. Joey watched it with a swelling heart as Bernhilda and Kurt exchanged their vows and rings, and the old bishop pronounced the blessing in a musical voice which seemed to reach to the farthest ends of the church. When the bridal was over, there followed the nuptial Mass, and Joey, as a Protestant, had to sit down, while the other maids followed bride and groom to the altar-rails to partake of it. Then the final solemn blessing was uttered; the organ pealed out joyfully, and, followed by her flower-like train of bride's-maidens, Bernhilda came

22

down the aisle on her young husband's arm, her face rosy with happiness and her eyes shining.

The register was signed and the kisses were given, and then they went to the sleighs to drive to the Kreide Hotel, where the wedding-dinner and reception were to take place.

Bernhilda moved among the guests, and Herr Mensch watched her with a wistful look in his eyes. He was devoted to his two pretty daughters, and Bernhilda was going so far away.

'You have Frieda still,' said Madge to him, later. 'You will have her for some years yet, Onkel Reise. And Gottfried and Gisela are not far distant. And think of the pleasure you and dear Tante Gretchen will have in going to visit Bernhilda in Lyons.'

'That is true, *mein Kind*,' he said, with a half-sigh. 'But it is hard to lose them, even when one knows that it will be for happiness.'

Then he cheered up as the Robin ran up to him, to claim him as partner for the dance which would finish up the main part of the festivities. Bernhilda and her bridegroom were put into the centre; the married couples formed a ring round them, while the unwedded paired off outside. To a merry tune, the dance went on, till, at a sign, Kurt clasped his bride and broke through the circles, bearing her with him to the door, where he released her to her mother and Tante Luise, and they vanished to change into travelling-dress for the honeymoon, which was to be spent in Vienna. The bridesmaids ran after to proffer their help, but, except for Frieda, Frau Mensch sent them away, and they went back to the *Rittersaal*, where music came from the orchestra and formed a soft accompaniment to the buzz of conversation that was going on. The bishop caught the Robin as she went past, and perched her on his knee and talked to her gravely. He loved children dearly, and she was rarely shy, so they got on very well. Wanda, her arm round her own little sister, was smiling at her young husband, and looking, so Jo thought, more like a fairy princess than ever. Maria Marani strayed away to chatter with some of her own friends, and Jo was left alone for a moment. She looked round to where Juliet was holding an animated conversation with another old girl, Grizel Cochrane, who had stayed on for the wedding, and decided that they wouldn't want to be interrupted. She drifted over to the door and peeped into the room where the wedding-presents were, but she had seen them before, and they held no special fascination for her at the moment. She was turning away, when she saw Gertlieb, the Mensches' servant, making her way towards them, her face white and frightened.

Jo ran forward. 'Gertlieb! What is it?' she asked imperatively.

'Madame,' gasped Gertlieb. 'Pray, Fräulein Joey, has Fräulein Bernhilda gone? For she said I was to say naught till they had left.'

'Not yet,' said Jo. 'What is wrong?'

'Madame is ill—suddenly,' sobbed Gertlieb, who had burst into frightened tears. 'She bid me fetch Herr Mensch, but not till the little bride had gone, for she would not mar her bridal.'

Joey thought rapidly. She knew that the old lady would never forgive anyone who upset Bernhilda in the moment of her bridal joy. At the same time, Herr Mensch would be anxious to hasten to the side of his mother—and old Frau Mensch was very old and very frail. Then her perplexity was solved, for a chorus of shouts told her that the young pair were saying 'farewell'.

'Stand back, Gertlieb,' she said. 'Go behind that palm. If Frau von Eschenau sees you, she will guess that something has gone wrong, and will stop.'

Still sobbing, Gertlieb hid behind the great branching palm, and when Bernhilda reached the doorway there was only Joey, rather white, but with a smile, to kiss her and wish her a very happy life.

The elder girl kissed the younger tenderly. 'Farewell, Joey,' she whispered. 'God keep thee.'

'Farewell,' said Joey.

The rest of the company followed, and, to a chorus of good wishes, Bernhilda and Kurt made their way to the street, where the sleigh was waiting to take them to the *Bahnhof*. There was a last kiss for the father and mother who had loved her so tenderly and cared for her all her life; a final waving of hands; a shower of rose-petals and silver horse-shoes; and Bernhilda was gone. Joey turned away, and sought her sister, her eyes bright with unshed tears, her face white with dread.

Madge exclaimed as she saw her little sister come to her

with that pallid face, 'Joey! What on earth is the matter? Are you ill?'

'It's old Frau Mensch—*die Grossmutter*,' sobbed Joey, breaking down at last. 'Gertlieb has come to say she is very ill, but Bernhilda was not to know. Oh, Madge, tell them for me!'

Madge whitened herself, but she kept her head. 'Of course, Joey. Don't cry, dearie, but find Jem for me, and ask him to get them away to another room. Dry your eyes, honey, or people will wonder what is wrong.'

Joey scrubbed her eyes fiercely with the back of her hand, since her handkerchief seemed to be missing at the moment, and went off to find Jem. He exclaimed, but nodded at once. 'Go and tell Madge to come to that little room in the corner, Jo. The guests will all be busy with the gifts and are not likely to notice.'

Joey went back to Madge, and presently Jem was to be seen with Herr Mensch in tow, while Frau Mensch had vanished. The girl went back to the palm behind which she had left Gertlieb, and found her still there, the undried tears glistening on her cheeks. 'My sister and brother have told them,' she said. 'You had better go home, Gertlieb.'

Gertlieb curtsied and slipped out at once, and Jo went to seek Frieda and Tante Luise. She must tell them, for it was unfair to leave it all to Madge. Frieda was in a corner with some of the other girls, laughing and talking, and Tante Luise was in the room where the gifts had been set out. Joey came up to the merry knot of school-girls, and her sorrowful face startled them.

Frieda jumped up from her seat and threw her arms round her. 'Don't look so sad, Joey. They will come to say "farewell" before they go to France, and Bernhilda has said that we are all to visit her in the holidays.'

'It isn't that,' said Joey, her lips quivering. 'But come with me, Frieda, will you?'

Greatly wondering, Frieda went with her into the hall, and there, behind a palm, Joey broke the news in her own way. 'Oh, Frieda! It's so horrid—and just when we were all so happy!'

'What is it?' asked Frieda, kissing her. 'Oh, Joey! There is nothing wrong with Baby David?'

Joey shook her head. 'No; he's all right. It's—it's *die Grossmutter*!'

Frieda looked at her. 'How do you know?' she demanded.

'Gertlieb came, but she wasn't to say anything till Bernie and Kurt had gone,' said poor Joey. 'I've told Madge, and she and Jem are telling your mother and father. Frieda, we must find Tante Luise. And oh! What shall we do with all these people?'

Frieda bit her lips to steady them. 'I will find Tante Luise,' she said at length. 'Don't cry, Joey. She will get well again—she *must*!'

Jem came out of the little room and went up to the leader of the orchestra. He spoke to him, and at once the music stopped, breaking off in the middle of a bar. All conversation ceased at this, and all eyes were turned to the musicians in amazement.

Jem took advantage of it at once. 'The family of our little bride are in grief,' he said simply. 'Herr Mensch's mother is very ill, and they have been summoned to her bedside. I deeply regret to have to ask you to leave us; but we are needed.'

Little exclamations of sympathy came from all over the room. People at once arose and made ready to depart. The musicians began to pack up their instruments, and in half an hour the great room was empty, save for a few servants and two of the Chalet School staff, who had stayed behind to pack up the gifts. Joey had gone with Frieda and Marie von Eschenau to the flat in the Mariahilfe, while the Maranis had taken off the Robin and Wolfram, the youngest of the Von Eschenau children. The rest had returned to their homes, and were waiting for news of the old lady. In the church where the marriage had taken place so happily, the bishop and the organist were kneeling, praying for God's help for the family. And in the quiet flat, old Frau Mensch was drifting away to the Paradise where Baby Natalie and her husband were awaiting her.

Towards six o'clock she stirred, and opened her eyes. 'Do not grieve,' she whispered. 'It is well.'

A minute later Jem laid down the tiny frail wrist he had been holding, and rose from his post with a look there was no mistaking.

But those who looked on the quiet face to which kindly death had restored something of its old-time beauty, knew that it was, indeed, well with her, and she had reached the baby daughter she had mourned so deeply.

Chapter V

EUSTACIA ARRIVES

'PENNY for them, Joey.'

'Not even sixpence! They're much too valuable!'

Mary Burnett, head-girl of the Chalet School, laughed, and tucked her hand into Jo's arm. 'The new girls ought to be here soon,' she said. 'Aren't there a lot for this term?'

'Thirteen,' said Jo solemnly. 'Five for us. And two of them are Dutch. We've never had Dutch girls before. I wonder what they will be like.'

'Just like everyone else,' retorted Mary. '*I* only hope they can speak something besides their own language. Won't it be awful if they can't?'

'Ghastly,' agreed Joe.

It was the Friday, and the School had come up from Innsbruck the previous day. Frieda had been left behind, to wait for her grandmother's funeral, which would take place on the Saturday afternoon.

Mary now swung Jo round to the window, and strolled over, talking of the coming term. 'My last,' said the head-girl, with a sigh. 'I hate the thought; but they do need me at home. At any rate I mean to see that it's a good term, Joey.'

'That's tempting the Fates,' retorted Joey. 'After that, I shouldn't wonder if we had whooping-cough and—and mumps, just to pay you out for being so sure!'

'Rubbish!' said Mary. 'Oh, Joey! There they come!'

She waved to the window, and Joey, pressing her nose against the panes, which had been treated with something to keep them from frosting over, saw a tall woman, followed by a file of girls, all marching towards the Chalet.

The new mistress was greeted by Mademoiselle, who sent a maid for Mary, Deira O'Hagan (an Irish girl), Paula von Rothenfels, Marie von Eschenau, and Joey Bettany.

'Mary, Gianetta, Arda, and Luise will sleep in the Amber room,' she said, singling them out. 'Deira, please take charge of these three.—Paula, I wish you and Marie to take these juniors and this girl, Dorothy Brentham, over to Le Petit Chalet. Tell Miss Wilson that these are her new girls.— Joey, these are Greta McDonald and Eustacia Benson. They sleep in the Violet room. Will you take them there, and show them where to put their things, please.'

The old girls shepherded their followers, and while Marie and Paula ran for coats and caps and boots, the others led the way upstairs. Deira went off to the Leaf room, once Miss Stewart's abode, with her three. Mary led hers to the Amber room.

Joey, with Greta and Eustacia in tow, made for the Violet room. Arrived, she pointed to two of the four beds there. 'Those are your beds,' she remarked. 'That one is Greta's, and this is Eustacia's. Those are your bureaux, where your clothes will be kept. We don't wash in our rooms, but in the splasheries—bathrooms, you know.'

'You are permitted to use slang here?' asked Eustacia.

Joey stared at her. 'That isn't slang,' she said abruptly. 'You'd better take off your things or you may catch cold in these warm rooms. The stove's been lighted because it's so cold today.'

'Most unhealthy,' replied Eustacia, her nose in the air. Then her eyes fell on her bed, and she uttered a little cry of horror. 'Feather beds! How insanitary! I must have a mattress! I *never* sleep on feathers!'

'You'll be glad to here,' replied Joey, with a grin. 'Between them, too. It gets jolly cold at nights, I can tell you!'

Greta, a shy child of thirteen, moved over to her little cubicle, with its dainty hangings of violet-sprayed material, and began to take off her hat and coat.

Joey went to her. 'These go downstairs in the cloak-room,' she said. 'Your shoes, too. Change now, and then, when we go down again, you can bring them with you and I'll show you where to put them.—And you had better do the same, Eustacia,' she went on, to the other occupant of the room.

But Eustacia made no attempt to remove her outdoor

garments. Instead, she stood looking round her, a distasteful expression on her face.

'Buck up,' said Joey impatiently, when Greta was nearly ready and the other child had made no move to prepare at all. 'It's not chilly up here, but it's not exactly warm. I've got heaps to do as well, and can't spend all my time dawdling about here. Besides, we're not supposed to, anyway.'

'I cannot sleep here,' said Eustacia decidedly. 'I must see the head-mistress and ask her to be so kind as to give me a room to myself. Also, I must have a mattress on which to sleep! and I must have proper ventilation.'

Joey's expression while she listened to this harangue was a picture. She was furious, disgusted, and dying to laugh, all at once. However, it was too soon to pull up the new girl for disrespect to a prefect, so she merely said, 'You can do that when you have changed. And we are expected to keep the rules here, so I'm afraid you must hurry up.'

Eustacia heaved a sigh, and removed her thick coat of the regulation brown, and her tam which matched it. Then she sat down on the side of the bed and took off her heavy boots. While she was busy, Joey had strolled to the window, and was looking out at the snow-covered scene. The Violet room looked up the valley towards the great Tiern Pass, and everywhere was white with snow. Only the pines stood up, black and bare against it. Up the valley lights were twinkling from the windows of the various chalets, for the short winter afternoon was drawing to a close. The stars were coming out, and a young moon was riding overhead. Greta came shyly, and stood beside her, and the prefect pointed out various landmarks while they waited for the other girl.

'I am ready now,' said Eustacia's voice behind them, and Joey turned round to survey the other girl.

She saw a slight child, with long fair hair, parted in the middle and plaited severely back from a high forehead. A pair of cold grey eyes met hers; and she noted a thin-lipped mouth and an obstinate chin. Her dearest could never have called Eustacia pretty; and yet it might have been possible. The thin lips were well-cut; and the short, straight nose was good. Joey had a vague idea that if the thick hair had been loosened it would show a natural wave which would have softened the severe face.

29

She turned to Greta. Here was something quite different. A pink face, with short fair hair curling round it; shy, blue eyes, and a babyish mouth, with dimples at the corners. Greta was very attractive, though Jo decided that she was shyer even than Simone Lecoutier had been during her first term. Even as she thought it, there came the sound of flying steps, and the young lady herself ran into the room.

'Joey! Mademoiselle says what make you up here so long?' Simone's English was apt to suffer when she was excited. 'You are to return to the common-room at once, and bring the new girls with you. *Kaffee und Kuchen* are almost ready, and Mary says that it is your night.'

'Bother!' said Joey. 'So 'tis! Well, grab your things, you two, and come on!' She slipped her arm through Simone's, and, followed by the new girls, they went downstairs, where a throng of school-girls of all ages met them with shouts of welcome to Jo and Simone, who were evidently popular.

Eustacia looked round her disparagingly. She was in a big, low room, with walls of pale green, on which were hung copies of pictures by good modern artists. Basket-chairs were scattered about on the polished floor in sociable groups, and, at one end of the room, was a green-painted table, on which stood cups and saucers and a huge urn. Baskets of buns and twists of bread were being handed about by younger girls, and a short, stocky senior, with pleasant face and merry smile, was busy at the urn. At sight of Joey she put down the cup she was filling, and remarking, 'Come on, an' do your own duty, you slacker!' strolled over to a merry group, where she subsided into a wicker chair.

'Take 'em over to those kids,' said Jo to Simone, indicating a cluster of the younger girls with a wave of her hand. 'Grab that wretched little Margie, and tell her she's to look after them. Evvy, too.' Then she left the two new lambs to their fate, and made for the urn and her duty.

'Come,' said Simone. She led Eustacia and Greta over to the group, singled out a girl of fourteen with a striking-looking face, and a fair-haired child of the same age, and said, 'These are two new girls, Margie and Evadne; Joey desires that you will guard them.'

'Like her nerve,' grumbled the girl addressed as 'Margia', 'Righto, Simone.—Come on, you two! Scrounge chairs from somewhere, and sit down.'

Greta meekly found herself a chair and sat down, but not Eustacia. Furious at being treated in this off-hand manner, she turned on the startled Margia, demanding, 'Where are your manners? Are we not in the position of your guests?'

Margia stared, and a gasp went up from the others.

'What cheek!' cried a pretty, dark girl, who was unmistakably English. 'D'you expect us to get up and curtsy to you, your Majesty?'

'But how rude,' added another, who was as unmistakably foreign. 'What, then, shall we do with this maiden, Margie?'

'Get her a chair or something—an' fall down an' worship her,' said Margia, who had recovered herself by this time. 'Look here, Eustacia—if that's your handle—take a bit of advice from me. Don't start off by bucking, even if you *are* someone to write home about at home. We are quite accustomed to that kind here. We've even had a princess, and lots of these folk have soppy titles——'

'And Margie has a clever pop—though you'd never think it to look at her,' put in the child Simone had addressed as 'Evadne'.

A laugh went round at this sally, but Margia continued her remarks unperturbed. 'And we don't think anything of even a duke, now. So get yourself a chair, an' take that coffee Kitty Burnett's holding for you, and sit down, and don't be a silly ass.'

Margia's tones were kinder than her words, but Eustacia was not accustomed to girls, and she was foolish enough to resent them. 'I shall appeal to the head-mistress,' she said furiously. 'I will not be treated with rudeness by a parcel of school-girls who mistake vulgarity for wit.'

The atmosphere changed at once, and she might have found herself in deep waters had not a watchful senior strolled up to the little group to make a few remarks. By the time her conversation with them was ended, a French child had pushed a chair towards Eustacia, and she was sitting in it, coffee in one hand, buttered twist in the other, and matters had calmed down for the time being.

Nevertheless, by bedtime, a good many people had heard of Eustacia's foolish threat to Margia and Evadne, and were inclined to look on this particular new girl with dislike.

Margia summed her up in the dormitory that night when

they were all undressing. 'So *that's* Eustacia Benson, is it? Well, all I have got to say is that she jolly well *looks* it! She's a sneaking smug prig, and she wants taking down at least *fifty* pegs before she'll be fit to live with!'

Chapter VI

TROUBLES BEGIN

By Monday morning every girl in the Chalet School had come to the conclusion that Eustacia Benson was no welcome addition to it.

'Of all the rotten little sneaks!' flamed Margia Stevens during break. She had been in trouble the previous evening, owing to Eustacia's calmly informing Mademoiselle that she had seen Margia Stevens drawing in her prayerbook during the service which was held for the Protestant girls in the little private chapel. Mademoiselle, somewhat startled by the information, had, unfortunately, acted on it, and Margia had been lectured on her iniquities, and sent to bed when the juniors went at half-past seven.

'She's a mean little prig,' said Elsie Carr, who was one of Margia's bosom friends.

'I do not like her,' sighed Simone Lecoutier. 'She says rude things about the beds.'

'But why?' demanded Ilonka Barkocz, a Hungarian of fourteen.

'Says they are insanitary,' said Suzanne Mercier briefly.

Margie looked round them. They were nearly all friends of long standing. Elsie Carr had come to the school the previous term, but she had fitted in with them comfortably, and she and Margia led the others by the nose; all save Simone, who had one adoration in the school—Joey Bettany.

'Joey was talking some rot this morning about it being the way she's been brought up,' said the leader of this promising coterie. 'Well, she's *here* to be brought up, and I vote we do it!'

The two Americans, Evadne Lannis and Cornelia

Flower, exchanged glances. Cornelia was being well and truly brought up by the others, and, since the days when she had been the naughtiest and most insubordinate girl the school had ever known, she had improved immensely.

'I'd just despise to be a rubber-necked fourflusher!' said Evadne, using expressions that would have called down the just wrath of those in authority if they had heard her.

Fortunately for her, they did not, though Margia frowned at her, and said sharply, 'You *know* Madame forbade you to say that.'

'Oh, can that!' retorted Evadne surprisingly.

This time Nemesis overtook her—deservedly. Mary Burnett happened to be passing, and she heard. She stood stock-still, and called Evadne to her. '*What* were you saying?' she asked frostily.

Evadne shuffled her feet and murmured something wholly unintelligible.

'What were you saying?' repeated Mary imperturbably.

Thus urged, Evadne mumbled the objectionable expression, and was requested to pay her due fine into the fines box.

'And I hope that will be the last for some time,' added Mary severely.

She turned away, and the episode would have dropped, had not a precise voice remarked approvingly, 'I agree with you, Mary. The slang Evadne uses is unladylike in the extreme.'

'Pray, who asked *you* to interfere?' demanded Mary, when she had recovered her breath. 'Attend to your own affairs, and leave Evadne to attend to hers. And, while I think about it, permit me to inform you that people who tell tales are not liked here, Eustacia. Don't do it again.' This time she did leave the middles, and they, with one accord, turned their backs on Eustacia, and gave vent to their opinions of her—none of them polite.

'Sneaking little cat!' cried Margia. 'One good thing, Mary settled her all right!'

'Thank goodness,' put in Elsie. 'At least the prees don't encourage tell-tales!'

'I would rather speak slang than speak as she does,' added Simone.

'Leave her to herself,' advised Cornelia. 'I'd despise to have anything to do with such a mean!'

33

They stalked off in a body, leaving Eustacia looking very black.

The bell rang for the return to lessons shortly after that, and the Fourth form, in which Eustacia found herself, retired to their form-room for a lesson on geography. Miss Wilson, who was Geography mistress, was a favourite with all the girls, and they enjoyed her lessons, which were always interesting.

Unluckily, Evadne was upset by the trouble with Mary, and was not disposed to work. Instead of putting contour-lines in her map of North America, she nudged Ilonka Barkocz, and the pair embarked on a game of noughts and crosses, played surreptitiously under the desk. Eustacia sat behind them, and once, while lifting her head to consider a moment, she caught sight of what they were doing. Her nose was tilted contemptuously at the sight, for Eustacia had a whole-hearted love for knowledge, though she was distinctly bored by this particular lesson. Geography had not entered very much into the scheme of her education so far, though in classics and mathematics she was remarkably well advanced and worked with the Fifth in both subjects. For all others she was in the Fourth, and would have been in the Third had it not been that Madge Russell had decided that, for a girl to take some subjects in the Fifth and others in the Third was rather ridiculous. Apart from that, the average age of the Third was nearly two years less than her own, while that of the Fourth was fourteen years five months, and Eustacia was fourteen years and two months.

'She isn't good enough all round for the Fifth,' said Madge, when she and the staff were discussing the matter. 'In some subjects she is far above the Fourth. Let her be Fourth for general things, and she must take classics and maths with the Fifth.'

The staff had agreed, so Eustacia, much to her own disgust, found herself with girls of her own age, instead of, as she had confidently expected, with the top form. This had been a grievance indeed, and she had even gone to Mademoiselle about it. Mademoiselle had given her short-shrift, pointing out that, since it was only in two subjects she was so good, while in most of the others her work did not compare too favourably with that of the Third, it was impossible to put her with girls whose classics and maths might not be so brilliant as her own, but who far surpassed her in general subjects and knowledge.

Finding the Head immovable on this point, Eustacia had left the study; but she nursed her wrath after the unpraiseworthy manner that was hers, and vented it on the innocent members of her form, who had already decided that they would rather have been without her. On this occasion she raised her hand, as she had been bidden after sundry skirmishes with Miss Maynard during the first part of the morning, and when Miss Wilson turned from helping Hilda Bhaer, she noticed it. 'What is it, Eustacia?' she asked briskly. 'Can't you get on? Bring your work here and let me see.'

'I am perfectly able to cope with this childish map-drawing,' said Eustacia calmly, while the rest of the form gasped at her temerity. 'It is only that I felt that you ought to know that the two girls in front of me are wasting their time in some babyish games insead of doing as they were bidden.'

Cornelia promptly emitted a long-drawn hiss at this blatant tale-bearing, and Evadne and Ilonka turned round to look at her with scorn in their faces.

As for Miss Wilson, she was so much surprised that, for a moment, she was left speechless. At length she rallied. 'That will do, Eustacia,' she said coldly. 'You may sit down. —Cornelia, do you wish to leave the room? If so, make that unpleasant noise again, and you will go to the study.— Go on with your work, girls, and let me have no more idling.—Eustacia, I will speak to you at the end of morning school.'

The work went on, even Evadne and Ilonka electing to attend to their maps. 'Bill' had taken no notice of the tale, but she might be moved to investigate on her own account. But though the girls were all busy, the pleasant atmosphere which usually accompanied these lessons was at an end. Miss Wilson spoke sharply when she addressed her class, and the girls themselves worked in utter silence, which somehow managed to carry with it the scorn they were all feeling for the informer.

When the lesson was over, Miss Wilson gathered up her books and left the room, only turning to remind Eustacia to come to her in the staff-room at the end of the morning. Eustacia rose in her seat, and bowed her head slightly as

35

she replied that she would remember. Then 'Bill' was gone, and Miss Stewart, the History mistress, came to take her place, so there was no time for anyone to say anything.

When the bell rang for the end of morning school, be sure that the Fourth made the most of their opportunity.

'Trot along to Bill and tell her some tales,' sneered Margia, as she picked up her books and made for her locker.

'Mind you tell her always about everything wicked we do!' added Evadne.

'Don't forget to say that we've been ragging you just now,' was Elsie's contribution.

'You hateful girls!' cried Eustacia.

'We may be hateful, but at the least we bear no tales,' said Ilonka.

Suzanne Mercier sniffed. 'She is not nice, this Eustacia. I find it better that we do not speak to her.'

'I agree,' said Margia. 'Do you hear, all of you! No one is to have anything to do with Eustacia Benson till she's apologised to Evadne and Ilonka for trying to get them into trouble.'

'I dont' care!' cried Eustacia furiously. 'I'm sure, it means nothing to *me* that you should be rude. I never met such ill-bred, unladylike girls, and I shall inform Miss Wilson of your abominable treatment of me!' The next moment she was sorry she had said that. The girls drew away from her.

A little smile edged Margia's lips. 'Yes; I suppose we might have expected that,' she said thoughtfully. 'But somehow, Eustacia, I don't expect you'll find Miss Wilson ready to listen to you. We don't encourage sneaks in this school, you know. Now, you'd better trot off, or Bill will have something to say to you for being late.'

'I shall tell her that, too!' shouted Eustacia, throwing all caution to the winds.

'I guess you will,' said Evadne. 'But it's stale news to her; I let it out myself, ages ago.'

There was a general laugh at this, for Evadne's 'letting out' had been quite involuntary on the part of both of those concerned. Miss Wilson had entered the form-room one day, to hear the small American announce the fact that she had not finished 'that *ghastly* chart Bill gave us to do!' Miss Wilson, being possessed of a sense of humour, had nearly laughed outright when Evadne turned round and grasped the fact that she must have heard. She had managed to keep a straight face, however, and had sent the young lady to her seat at once. At the end of the lesson, Evadne had followed her out of the room and apologised, confusedly explaining that she hadn't meant to be rude. 'Oh, it was my old name at the School of Economics,' Miss Wilson had said lightly. 'It was quite like old times to hear it again. I knew you had no idea of being rude, Evadne; but do, my dear girl, try to get out of the way of screeching so loudly if you don't want us to know your pet-names for us.' So when Eustacia announced her intention of informing Miss Wilson of what they called her, the Fourth was wildly hilarious.

The new girl shut the lid of her locker with a bang, and stalked out of the room, her nose in the air. Margia waited till the door had closed behind her, and then summoned the others for a palaver, irrespective of the fact that they should all have been making their way to the splasheries, to get ready for *Mittagessen*.

'She's a rotten little sneak and spy and prig,' she said hurriedly, with one eye on the door in case anyone in authority should come in and catch them. 'It's about time she knew how we look on such piggish ways; so remember, no one is to speak to her, or have anything to do with her.'

They all agreed, and then streamed off at top-speed to make up for lost time.

Meanwhile Eustacia was having her interview with Miss Wilson, and not liking it at all.

'Why did you tell tales this morning, Eustacia?' she asked gravely, tackling the question at once.

'I considered that you ought to know that Evadne and Ilonka were wasting time,' replied Eustacia priggishly.

'That may be so. But surely you must have realised that I could not possibly take any notice of tale-bearing?' said Miss Wilson. 'The girls would have little respect for me if I did.'

'Does that matter?' asked Eustacia. 'I should have

37

thought that the discipline was the first thing to be considered.'

'Don't be impertinent,' said Miss Wilson sharply. 'Of course it matters. If a mistress has to depend on sneaking for her discipline, then the sooner she realises her unfitness for teaching, and gives up the work, the better for all concerned!'

Eustacia looked politely contemptuous, but she said nothing.

Miss Wilson looked at her, and frowned impatiently. How was she to impress on this child the meanness of what she had done? 'Cannot you understand, Eustacia?' she said. 'In a boys' school you would have been thrashed well by one of the fellows, and everyone would say it served you right. I do not imagine that the girls here will proceed to such lengths, but I am afraid you are making things hard for yourself. We have never permitted tale-bearing, and the girls were all horrified at what you said.'

'I cannot help that,' returned Eustacia. 'I must do my duty.'

'By all means,' said the mistress. 'But it is *not* your duty to interfere between the girls and me. You took too much on yourself, and were officious, to say the least of it. Apart from that, let me assure you that neither I nor any other mistress in this school will, for one moment, listen to tale-bearing, and you may make up your mind to that.'

'Indeed?' said Eustacia.

Now Miss Wilson had been exceedingly forbearing, but that final comment destroyed the last remnant of her patience. Rising from her seat, she looked down at the child before her. 'I warned you before of impertinence,' she said sternly. 'I shall not repeat that warning again. Now go; but be sure that the girls will not let you off easily, and I doubt if prefects or staff will wish to help you. You are so much wrapped up in yourself that you seem determined not to recognise the fact that others have their rights. School-girls, you will find, are as strict as their brothers in matters of honour—and rightly so.'

'I am honourable!' exclaimed Eustacia, roused from her scornful attitude at last. 'How dare you say I am not?'

'How dare *you* use such a tone in addressing a mistress? It is well for you that we know something of your story, and are able to make allowances for you. Now go. No; not another word, unless you wish to apologise for your rudeness.'

That last, Eustacia was not prepared to do—and she dared not say what she felt in the face of the mistress's severity; so she left the room, boiling with rage, and feeling that never had any girl been so unhappy before.

Chapter VII

THE PREFECTS TAKE A HAND

NEEDLESS to state, the story was all over the School before the end of the afternoon. The Fourth were not very likely to keep it to themselves, and they passed it on to the Third, who communicated it to the 'babies', as they all called the juniors. From them, it came by way of Robin Humphries, Peggy Burnett, and Irma von Rothenfels to the seniors, who were duly horrified.

'What a little horror she must be!' said Joey Bettany cheerfully.

'It is not the first time she has told tales,' observed Simone.

'D'you mean about Margie last night?' asked Jo. 'I know that, of course. I thought it was just an unexpected break on her part—like being so frightfully religious she thought it blasphemous to draw during service. Of course, Margie's an idiot to do it; still, it wasn't exactly cricket to get her into trouble over it.'

'Not only that,' said Simone. 'For this morning she interfered when Mary reproved Evadne for using slang.—Is it not so, Mary?'

'It is,' said Mary shortly.

'Go on; tell us what she said,' said Joey with interest.

Mary shrugged her shoulders. 'She was impertinent,' she said.

However, those who had not been there at the time were not going to be put off in this way, so Simone described what had occurred, and the rest of the Fifth and Sixth listened with lively interest.

'What can we do about it?' asked Marie von Eschenau.

'I don't see that we can do anything,' said Mary, frowning. 'Of course, if she comes telling tales to us, we can squash her; but we can't take any notice otherwise.'

'Let's get on with school affairs, shall we?—Mary, what about a meeting tonight?' Deira asked.

'I suppose we'd better have one,' replied Mary. 'Very well, you people, prees' meeting at eighteen o'clock. Mind you are punctual, for there's a good deal to discuss.'

'When isn't there?' asked Joey, balancing herself on one leg and trying to put the toe of the other foot on the top-shelf of the book-shelves. She overbalanced next minute; grabbed at Deira, who stood nearest and was not prepared for it, and the two went down with a crash, involving Simone, Marie, and Biana di Ferrara in their downfall. By the time they had got themselves sorted out, the bell was ringing for *Kaffee und Kuchen*, and they had to smooth their hair and go off to the *Speisesaal*.

'It still snows,' said Simone, as they passed the long window in the passage.

'Wonder when it will stop,' said Joey. 'We haven't been out for three days now, and I'm bored with the house.'

'Perhaps tomorrow,' suggested Bianca. 'Then we can have a snow-fight.'

'Oh, good! And if we can, let's get Mademoiselle to ring up the Saints and ask them to meet us in the water meadows at Seespitz, and have a battle there,' laughed Deira.

'Wouldn't it be fun? They'll want to hear all about the wedding, too,' began Marie. Then she stopped as she remembered what had followed the wedding.

The others guessed at once what she was thinking, and Joey hastened to say, 'That would be a splendid idea. And we might ask Mademoiselle to let us give them coffee and cake, too!'

'Have to collect, then,' said Deira, as they entered the *Speisesaal*, where most of the middles were awaiting them.

It was only at the week-end that the juniors came over to join them for this meal, though they were present at *Mittagessen* unless the weather was very bad. While anxious to keep the little girls to their own quarters, the Heads of the Chalet School felt that it was only right that the seniors should have a certain amount to do with them, and arranged matters this way.

Conversation was desultory, and then someone noticed that Eustacia Benson was not in the room.

'Does anyone know where Eustacia is?' asked Deira, who had made this discovery first.

Everyone stared round, and finally Suzanne Mercier hazarded the suggestion that she might be in the splasheries. She had upset some ink that afternoon, and her hands had been a sight to behold.

'She may be trying to get them clean,' said Suzanne.

'What on earth was she doing to spill ink?' asked Joey interestedly; while Mary sent one of the younger middles to seek Eustacia, and tell her to hurry up.

'She fell over the ink-can,' said Cyrilla Maurús, a country-woman of Ilonka's. 'It really was not my fault, Joey. I had set it down in the corner, and I could not know that she was going there. She tripped over some books, and fell all her length, and caught at the ink-can with her hands. The ink went all over—even on her face.'

'Didn't she look funny?' said Maria Marani, with a delighted chuckle. 'And she was so angry, Joey. She said she . . . nothing,' she tailed off lamely, as a sudden remembrance of the fact that Joey was now a full-blown prefect came to her.

Jo knew better than to pay any heed to Maria's speech, so she turned the conversation by asking who had anything ready for that term's number of *The Chaletian*, the school magazine, of which she was editress.

Meanwhile, Kitty Burnett had gone to the splasheries, and returned to say that she couldn't find Eustacia anywhere there.

'Then she must have gone up to her dormy, tiresome child!' said Mary sharply. 'Run upstairs and see, Kit. If she is still there, tell her about dormitory rules, and say she is to come down at once. Anyway,' she went on turning to her own peers, 'she *must* have heard the bell for *Kaffee und Kuchen*.'

Kitty obediently went off, but came back a little later on to say that Eustacia was not there.

Where *can* she be?' exclaimed Mary, beginning to look troubled. 'Jo, can you think?'

Joey shook her head. 'Music-rooms—library?' she suggested.

'The music-rooms were all empty at four, and you know

41

as well as I do that the library is still locked, as we haven't had time to see about the new books.'

'Then I don't know where she can be. You don't suppose she's been mad enough to go out?'

'Talk sense!' cried Deira. 'The chances are she's in some other dormy.—Come along, Paula, and we'll hunt through them and see.'

Deira and Paula went off, only to return, saying that Eustacia was nowhere to be found.

'Where *can* she be?' cried Mary, thunderstruck. 'Are you *sure* you've looked in all the dormies, you two?'

'We've even ventured into the staff-bedrooms,' said Deira. 'I thought it better to do so at once. She's such a queer kid, you never know what she might take it into her head to do.'

'We'd better tell Mademoiselle,' began Mary slowly; but she was interrupted by Joey.

'Better look into the music-rooms and the library first. No need to scare anyone till we must.'

'We *did* look into the music-rooms as we came past,' said Paula; 'but the library—that is locked, my dear Jo.'

'I know; but there's nothing to prevent her turning the key and going in, is there?' asked Joey.

'Only the fact that you have the key yourself in your desk,' said Deira drily. 'Don't you remember? You said you'd keep it, so that the middles shouldn't be tempted to go in till it was all ready.'

'So I did. Then where on earth can she be?'

There was a startled silence. The girls looked at each other.

'Kitchen?' suggested Simone at length.

'Not if Luise has anything to do with it,' replied Joey. 'Besides, *can* you see the great Miss Benson hobnobbing with the maids? 'Cos I *can't*!'

At this point Margia sneezed, and searching for her handkerchief, discovered that it was a minus quantity, and left the room to get one. Two minutes later she bounced back to announce breathlessly, 'There's a light on in the library!'

'Rats!' said Joey incredulously. 'How could there be? I have the only key.'

'There *is*! I saw it under the door!' declared Margia.

Joey got up. 'You're dreaming,' she said; 'but, all the same, I'll go and see.'

'I'm *not*!' Margia was indignant.

'Keep your hair on,' said the librarian soothingly. 'Coming, Mary?'

Mary nodded, and followed her out of the room. Deira, Paula, Bianca, and Maria came too. They streamed along the narrow passage, and came to the door marked 'Library'. Arrived there, Joey stopped, and pointed to the light gleaming through the crack at the back of the door.

'I told you so!' said Margia, who had accompanied her.

'If this is Miss Eustacia's doing, I'll have something to say to her,' observed Joey grimly, as she turned the handle.

The door opened, and they pressed in. There, sitting in a comfortable chair, her big coat wrapped round her, since the stove was not lighted, sat Eustacia, buried in a book. As they entered, she looked up, a frown of annoyance settling on her face. 'Oh, bother! Have *you* come?' she said crossly.

Hands in her blazer-pockets, Jo stalked across the room. 'I'll have my key, thank you,' she said tersely.

Eustacia started, and flushed pink. 'Oh, I forgot you might need it!' She took it out of a pocket, and dropped it into Jo's outstretched hand.

'Thank you,' said that young lady. 'And now, you can put that book back where you got it, and get out of this. I'll see you in the prefects' room at half-past seventeen.'

'Please don't be so absurd,' said Eustacia frostily. 'I have only just begun, and there is more than half an hour yet before half-past five.'

'Put that book back where you got it,' repeated Jo implacably. 'You have no business in here. It was locked for a purpose—but I'll speak to you about that later. At present, all *you* have to do is to come out as you are told, and go to *Kaffee und Kuchen*.'

'I do not desire food,' replied Eustacia. 'It is unnecessary to eat oftener than three times in the day, and I prefer to read.'

Mary decided that it was time for her to take a hand, for Joey looked ready to choke.

'You cannot read now, Eustacia,' she said firmly. 'It is against the rules. Please come at once, and don't be tiresome.'

Thus adjured, Eustacia reluctantly closed her book and tucked it under her arm.

'Put that book back in its proper place,' said Jo.

'Nonsense! I desire to borrow it. I will do it no harm, and it is unlikely that anyone else in the school would enjoy anything so erudite,' retorted Eustacia.

For reply, Joey snatched the book from her and glanced at it to see what it was. As she read its title her eyes widened—though not with wonder, as Eustacia confidently hoped. Instead, she swung round, anger flaming in her black eyes, exclaiming, 'How dare you touch the staff shelves? You can't say you didn't *know* they were staff, 'cos it's written up above them, and the notice saying that no girl is to borrow from them unless with special permission from the staff.'

'That will do, Joey,' said Mary quietly. 'We can't talk here—it's much too cold. Put the book away, and come out, all of you.'

Joey did as she was asked, and then left the room, carefully relocking the door, and putting the key into her blazer-pocket. They went back along the corridor to the warm, brightly-lit *Speisesaal*, where Mary poured out coffee for Eustacia and insisted on her drinking it. Joey went off to sit with Simone, the ever-faithful, and Marie von Eschenau, and the meal went on quietly. The others were dying to know what had happened, but with the seniors looking like that, didn't care to ask. Margia, who might have relieved their curiosity, was detained by Mary and Deira and warned to say nothing till they gave her permission. That *something* had happened was obvious, but there was no one to tell, and no one had any idea of addressing the girl who had broken the strict law of school-girl honour. As for Eustacia, she drank her coffee and ate her cakes with lowering brow. She had done nothing wrong, so far as she could see. Of course, she might have broken a rule, but, after all, she was new, and no one could expect her to know all the rules at once. She was not in the least sorry for what she had done; but she was angry at being turned out of the library and at Joey's tone to her.

Kaffee over, the girls scattered to their various pursuits till the bell should ring for preparation, and the prefects retired to the prefects' room to discuss what they should do with Eustacia.

'It was downright cheek,' declared Deira. 'And the way she spoke to Joey—a prefect—was the limit! It's high time someone told her that she isn't anyone in particular here. I'd be doing it myself with all the pleasure in life!'

'She's the edge!' said Joey gloomily, perching herself on the table. '*I* don't know what to do with her. And she's so beastly righteous with it all—little prig!'

In her perturbation, Mary let this unparliamentary language pass. 'We *must* settle her somehow,' she said in worried tones.

'True for you,' said Deria. 'The question is—how?'

'Lines?' suggested Marie.

Jo shook her head. 'I don't think that would meet the case. Besides, as likely as not she'd refuse to do 'em. No; it must be something different—something she'd mind more. And she must have sneaked the key out of my desk. It was there at fourteen this afternoon, I know, 'cos I saw it. We can't have that sort of thing going on. No; we must think of something better than lines.'

'Should we report her?' asked Simone, with a frown.

Mary shook her head. 'Not if we can possibly avoid it. She wouldn't understand the difference between reporting and sneaking, and she'd only say that we were doing what we're all so down on.'

'Let us say that she is not to use the library till half-term,' suggested Bianca brilliantly.

They fell on her with shrieks of joy. 'The very thing!' 'Bianca, you're a genius!' 'Just the best punishment of all for her!'

'And,' added Joey, with the first grin she had shown since the affair had begun, 'it really *is* making the punishment fit the crime—and I do like to do that when I can.'

So it was decided. They would hear what Eustacia had to say for herself—though no one could see how she could possibly explain the taking of the key from Jo Bettany's desk—and then, unless something quite unforeseen cropped up, they would banish her from the library until half-term.

'Half-past,' said Mary, consulting her watch when this was settled. 'She ought to be here by now. We'll give her five minutes more, and then, if she doesn't come, someone must go and fetch her.—You might, Carla.'

Quiet Carla von Flügen assented, and the prefects sat in silence for another five minutes.

Then Mary looked at her watch again and nodded. 'Go and fetch her, Carla. Of course, if any of the staff have her, it's not her fault, and you must wait till they're done. But I don't think it's likely. She doesn't have remedials at this time, and no one bothers about us, as a rule, till prep.'

Carla got up, and went to the door. 'What if she will not come?' she questioned, ere she opened it.

'Then *bring* her,' said Joey, with a grin. 'You're a lot bigger than she is, and she's all flab—no muscle anywhere. You'll have to treat her as if she were Robin if she behaves like it—though the Robin would never dream of being disobedient, anyhow.'

Carla opened the door, and at that moment they heard footsteps coming along the corridor.

The next moment Eustacia appeared on the scene and walked calmly past the startled sub-prefect who had been going to seek her, and marched up to the table round which they were all sitting. 'Well?' she said.

Chapter VIII

BEFORE THE PREFECTS

MARY turned and looked at the clock. 'You are late,' she said coldly. 'Were any of the staff detaining you?'

'No; but I was reading and overlooked the time,' Eustacia informed her coolly.

'Well, another time when we tell you to be here at a certain time, will you kindly see that you are?' replied the head-girl. Then she turned to Joey.—'I think you wished to speak to Eustacia, Josephine?'

Joey nodded. 'Where did you get the key of the library?' she asked.

'Out of your desk,' returned Eustacia. 'I overheard you say that you had put it there, so when I felt that I must read, I went and took it. I had intended to replace it when I was finished, of course.'

'How am I to know that?' Joey's voice was icy, and the laughter that usually informed it had vanished. 'You go to my desk, steal a key for which I am responsible, and, in spite of the fact that you are well aware that no one is to be permitted to use the library for some days yet, you go in. Now, what have you to say?'

'I did *not* steal the key!' said Eustacia passionately. 'How *dare* you say that to me?'

'No? Then what else do you call it?' demanded Jo.

'I borrowed it.'

'Without first asking my permission. I should call that sort of thing stealing, anyhow.'

'I did *not* steal it!' repeated Eustacia. 'I should have put it back. How dare you accuse me of anything so dishonourable?'

'Well, I'm afraid you haven't shown yourself very honourable so far.'

Eustacia's lip curled. 'Oh, I see. Because I report girls who are breaking the rules——'

'And what about yourself?' queried Mary suddenly. '*You* were breaking the rules—and breaking them far more flagrantly than any of the girls you have sneaked about.'

'It was a foolish rule, so far as I am concerned.'

'Sorry; but I'm afraid that a rule is a rule, whoever comes up against it. Also, I advise you to speak more civilly. You aren't doing yourself any good by behaving like this, you know. Now—no; leave this to me, Joey—you have acted meanly and unfairly. What do you suppose would have happened if anyone in authority had asked Jo for that key and she had been unable to produce it?'

'I should, of course, have explained that I was compelled to borrow it.'

'Afraid that wouldn't have helped you,' said Mary briskly. 'No, Eustacia! It's no use trying to blink facts. Your behaviour has been all wrong, and I advise you to try again and see if you can't remove from our minds the very unpleasant impression you have left. And, apart from taking the key when you knew—you *must* have known—that it was forbidden, and reading in the library after it had been closed to everyone, why, may I ask, did you use a book from the staff shelves? As you were reminded at the time, there is a notice up, stating that no one is to use those books unless given special permission by the staff. You admitted that you had seen it. Do you think it was put there for fun?'

47

'I did not see that it need apply to me. I have been accustomed to have access to any book in my father's library, and I should not mark or harm them as an *ordinary* girl might do. I daresay many of these foreigners have no idea how to treat books——'

'Less about foreigners, if you please!' struck in Deira. 'I don't know if you realise that this is not England; still, in case you haven't, it's Austria, and the foreigners are not the Austrians.'

Mary cast a glance at her. Deira was hot-tempered, and she had no wish for an unpleasant scene.

Joey took the opportunity. 'Well, all this is beside the point. What does matter is that Eustacia Benson has seen fit to break rules right and left—although she's so keen to report other girls she catches at that very thing!' There was angry sarcasm in her voice, and Eustacia went pink again. All that remains is to tell her what her punishment is going to be.'

'Absurd!' said Eustacia. 'Girls like you cannot have the power to punish me.'

'Oh, we have—within certain limits,' Mary assured her. 'We are going to exercise those powers at once. Until half-term you will not be allowed to use the library.'

'It's unfair!' cried Eustacia passionately. 'I will not put up with it! I shall appeal to the head-mistress!'

'I shouldn't advise you to do that,' said Joey. 'You see, it won't be of any use, for Mademoiselle will only back us up, as it's a fair punishment. You chose to use the library in forbidden times, so we punish you by forbidding you to use it at the proper times. And if you *do* go to her, she will want to hear the whole story, and however you put it, I don't think you can make it sound a *pretty* story. You go to a senior's desk, and take from it a key that is not yours.'

'I have told you several times already that I meant to return it in due course!' interrupted Eustacia furiously.

'Well, even so, it doesn't make it any better. And another thing, will you kindly remember that we are prefects, and you may not speak to us like that?'

'I shall speak as I like!' For once, Eustacia was fully aroused. She hated these big, self-assured girls, who seemed so certain that they had the right to punish her as if she

48

were a mere baby. She hated the others, who would have nothing to do with her, just because she had followed her own sense of duty and reported them for wrong-doing. She knew, in her inmost heart, that she had not been in the right when she had abstracted that key and taken down that book from the forbidden shelves. She would let them know that she was not going to be treated in this manner. 'What are you but silly, empty-headed girls, with no true conception of the beauty of learning? What do *you* know of education and its marvellous benefits? You are worse than the children in the board-schools! I——'

The next moment she was seized in a strong grip, given a slight shake, and sat down abruptly in a chair, and Deira O'Hagan was standing over her. 'That's quite enough,' said Deira's voice. 'Now stop that nonsense, you silly little ass. Do you want to go into hysterics?'

Deira's actions and words were drastic, but they had their effect. The shake had recalled the excited girl to her senses, and made her realise what she was doing and saying. She turned on the others a face white as a sheet. Mary, thinking she felt faint, gave an exclamation, and turned to look for water.

But Eustacia was not faint. She was merely so angry that she could scarcely steady her voice to speak. With a mighty effort she managed it. 'You may think you can master me,' she said, speaking in low tones, 'but I will let you see that you cannot. I never wanted to come here—it was my cruel aunt who forced it on me, after she had gained control over me when my parents died. Well, I must stay here, for I have no money to take me away. But I'll make you all regret the day you ill-used and abused me, and I'll pay each one of you out for this.'

The girls heard her with startled ears. Then, at the pronouncement of this deadly feud, Joey Bettany suddenly lost her self-control, and, leaning back in her chair, she laughed till the tears ran down her cheeks. The others joined in, even Mary the steady, and Eustacia sat and glared at them.

'Ow—*ow*! I'm aching!' Joey sat up and mopped her eyes hilariously. 'Oh, Eustacia, you utter little *idiot*! Go away, and don't be so melodramatic again, or you'll be the death of us all! I'm sore with laughing!'

The others began to recover themselves, and then Mary pulled herself together. 'There is the bell for prep. Go

49

downstairs, Eustacia, and remember; when the library is opened again, you may not use it at until half-term. If we find you in it, or you are reported to us for being there, the matter will have to go to Mademoiselle, and, as I said, that won't be pleasant for you.'

Eustacia rose to her feet. 'Oh, you may laugh!' she said. 'You may be as scornful, as mocking, as you like! But you'll find out that it was not a mere threat. I will pay you all back for your treatment of me today, and you'll be sorry before I've finished.'

Mary's face grew serious. 'Eustacia,' she said quietly, 'remember that you may only make things considerably worse for yourself. And as for this silly, un-Christian talk of "paying back", just forget about it. That is all.'

Eustacia marched away, but she had not forgotten. Hers was a tenacious mind, and she meant to keep her word and revenge herself on these girls who had laughed at her and dared to shut her out of their precious library.

As for the prefects, when they were once more alone they looked at each other rather uncomfortably.

'I wish we had managed not to laugh,' said Mary at last. 'I'm afraid we have hurt her feelings.'

'Oh, rats!' said Joey. ' "Hurt her feelings", indeed! If she got what she deserves she'd get a good spanking! She talks like a silly baby! And if ever I catch her in the library again, to Mademoiselle I go, whether it gets her into a fiendish row or not!'

Deira looked sober. Once upon a time *she* had taken revenge into her own hands, and it had nearly brought about a tragedy. She would never forget that, and she wondered if she ought to interfere with Eustacia. Then she decided that *she* was possessed of a temper both hot and quick, while Eustacia, it seemed, was not given to flaring up often as she had done that evening.

'I do things without thinking,' thought Deira with humility. 'I don't think Eustacia is like that. Indeed, I'm sure she isn't. She'll be all right when she's had time to cool down a little, and when she learns that she isn't the *only* member of the human race on earth. I'll leave it. I might do more harm than good if I interfered.'

At the same time she resolved to keep an eye on the girl. But what Deira did not understand was that when a naturally cold temper is aroused it takes a long time to cool again, and that people like that may go to further ends than the hot-tempered folk who flare up and then calm down again. Eustacia had never been so angry in her life. It was going to be a difficult matter for her to forget her anger, and much was to happen before then.

Chapter IX

THE FOURTH TAKE ACTION

FOR a whole week the Fourth kept to their resolve, and not one of them spoke to Eustacia all that time. The Third followed their example the day after all the trouble, when the new girl 'reported' Kitty Burnett for using slang. Accordingly, Eustacia found herself severely ostracised, and, strangely enough, found it very unpleasant. Indeed, there were times when she longed for the jolly little home in Devonshire.

When Sunday came, Margia lifted the embargo she had placed on her own set, and Kitty followed her example. Thus, Eustacia found that the girls said 'Good-morning' to her when she entered the big common-room that morning, and Evadne even volunteered the information that, since it had ceased to snow *at last*, they were going for a long walk up the valley. Eustacia made no reply to anyone. She pushed past Evadne to the stove, where she stood, shivering and trying to warm herself. The silly child, thinking that she knew better than anyone else, had taken to discarding her big plumeau after she had got into bed, and slept under the blankets, which were all that remained. As a result, she was never warm at night, and, since the Violet dormitory was a peaceable one, no one in authority had found out about it as yet. This morning, however, she was to be discovered, for, since she had risen late, she had forgotten to lift the plumeau from the floor where she tossed it each night before she got into bed, and Matron, going on her rounds to see that all beds were being thoroughly aired and the rooms were as tidy as possible, found it where she had left it, and made up her mind to know, the minute breakfast was over, why it was there.

The bell went, and the girls streamed in to *Frühstück*. Since it was Sunday, they might use their own languages, and Eustacia, sitting between Anita Rincini and Giovanna Donati, with two French girls and a Norwegian facing her, had a dull time for the greater part of the meal. It is true that Anita and Giovanna occasionally remembered to address a sentence or two to her in English, but they were Fifth form and had their own concerns to interest them. As for the other three, they forgot the English child altogether and were deep in their own affairs. Eustacia, sitting eating primly of porridge, followed by eggs and rolls and honey, thought to herself that she hated this school more and more as the days went past. Most of the other new girls were beginning to feel their feet by this time, and to fit into one or other of the numerous little coteries and cliques always to be found in a girls' school, even shy Greta becoming friendly with Simone Lecoutier and Amy Stevens, sister of Margia of the Fourth. But there seemed to be no place for the daughter of the late professor, and Eustacia resented it fiercely. That it was largely her own fault was a thing she would never have allowed for one moment. She blamed the others, thinking that they were very unfair to her.

'More coffee, Eustacia?' asked Mary Burnett, at this point of her thoughts.

'I thank you—no,' said Eustacia frostily.

'Have a little more honey with your roll,' suggested Anita Rincini, offering the dish as she spoke.

'I have had enough,' replied Eustacia.

The door opened at this moment, to admit a tall fair girl, dressed in blue, and a general cry of 'Juliet!' rose at sight of her.

She laughed, and came forward. '*Guten Morgen*. Mademoiselle, may I have breakfast? We set out at five o'clock, Eigen and I, and I'm hungry. I thought I'd like a Sunday at school again.'

'Of course, have breakfast, my child,' said Mademoiselle, her kind face beaming with pleasure. 'How long do you stay, Juliette?'

'As long as you'll have me—Thank you, Rosa—a week, at least,' laughed Juliet, as she set to work on her porridge.

The meal was finished in leisurely fashion, and then

Mademoiselle rose. 'There will be no service at all this morning,' she said. 'Instead, we will all have a long walk up the valley, and return for *Mittagessen* early. After *Mittagessen* we will go out again, until it is time for *Kaffee und Kuchen*. This evening we will hold little services of our own. Will you all hasten with your bed-making, so that we may set out as soon as possible?' She then said grace, and the girls hurried off to their duties.

Eustacia went as slowly as possible, and was caught by Matron, last to leave the room. 'One moment, Eustacia. I am coming to your dormitory with you.'

Wondering what was going to happen, Eustacia followed the small, bustling lady, who ruled over the domestic side of the school, without a word. When they reached her cubicle she caught sight of her plumeau on the floor, and guessed what was coming.

'Why is your plumeau there, may I ask?' demanded Matron. 'Do you suppose you can have a fresh cover every week? Why could you not put it over the rail? Are you too lazy—or what?'

'I disapprove of these most insanitary things,' began Eustacia, but that was as far as she got.'

Matron interrupted her at once. 'That is no answer to my question. As to what you approve or disapprove, that doesn't matter here. Pick up that thing at once and hang it over the rail.'

Eustacia did as she was bidden, and the tyrant continued, 'And now, why couldn't you do that at first?'

'I forgot I had left it there,' said Eustacia loftily. 'These little accidents are liable to happen to anyone.'

'No impertinence!' snapped Matron, who had not had much to do with Eustacia so far, and really thought she was trying to be funny. 'What do you mean—you forgot?'

'I arose late,' explained Eustacia with dignity. 'I forgot that I had not picked up my—that thing—from the floor, and so you found it.'

'But what was it *doing* on the floor?' demanded Matron.

'I—er—put it there.'

'And why, pray?'

'Because I consider such things most insanitary,' replied Eustacia.

Matron stared at her. 'You seem to me to be bereft of your senses,' she said at length. 'Who, may I ask, gave you the right to say what is or is not insanitary? *When* did you put it there?'

'Last night, when I went to bed.' Eustacia, whatever her faults, had plenty of courage—and it required courage to face Matron in her present mood.

'You must have taken leave of your senses!' declared that lady, when she had found her breath again. 'Well, I'll take good care that *this* doesn't happen again. Pick up that plumeau and make your bed at once. I'll see you this evening.'

Then she took her departure, leaving behind her an aggrieved Eustacia, who made her bed as badly as usual —she had never done such a thing before coming to school —and left the room to seek a book and a corner. In that she was promptly frustrated by Miss Wilson, who sent her to the cloak-room to get ready for the walk, and refused to listen to any remarks on the subject.

Eustacia was growing furious again. In common with many bookish people she had a hatred of exercise, and loathed the idea of a long walk. Since she had come to the Tyrol such a thing had been impossible before, owing to the weather. Today, when the others were rejoicing in the fact that the snow had ceased to fall, she was glooming in a corner, putting on her high boots as slowly as she could.

'Buck up,' remarked Margia, seeing her. 'We're all ready, and you'll keep us waiting if you go at it as slowly as that. Where are your hat and coat?—Get them, Elsie, and hold them ready while I hunt up her gloves.—Look round for her scarf, Ilonka.'

'Kindly let my things alone!' snapped Eustacia.

'Come along,' said Elsie impatiently. 'Get into your coat.'

For reply, Eustacia snatched the coat from her and shook it well, before beginning to don it as slowly as she dared. She spent at least three minutes in fastening it, and another two in putting on her cap to her satisfaction. But over the scarf they nearly had a battle royal. She twisted it round her neck, and held out her hand for her gloves.

'I say, you can't go with your scarf like that,' said Cornelia. 'We all have to wear them crossed over our chests. Let Lonny fix yours for you.'

Ilonka came forward to do as she was asked, but as she took hold of one end, Eustacia whisked it indignantly away.

54

'I will certainly not go out looking as though I were a slum-child,' she said.

'Slum-child? But what is that?' asked Ilonka.

'Slum-child be bothered!' exclaimed Evadne. 'I guess you'll precious soon find out that you have to do as we all do here.'

Eustacia turned round, her head cocked a little more in the air than usual, and stalked to the door. At that moment Kitty Burnett rose from her stooping position—she had been making sure that her boot-laces were tight—and cannoned into her. Eustacia staggered and nearly fell, and Kitty began to stammer an apology. The rest, needless to say, broke into delighted giggles, which, however, changed to gasps of horror when Eustacia, so angry that she scarcely knew what she was doing, took a step forward and boxed Kitty's ears soundly.

Kitty roared, for the blow was a hard one.

'There!' panted Eustacia. 'That will teach you to stop making fun of me, you horrid little thing!'

The next moment she was almost overwhelmed by a torrent of indignant reproaches from the others.

'You *beast*!' exclaimed Margia, with an arm round Kitty's shoulders.—'There! Don't cry, Kitty, dear! We'll go to Matron and get her to put something on.'

'You—you *scum*!' gasped Evadne, when she had rapidly searched round her vocabulary and discarded most of the things that came into her head.

'*Méchante!*' pronounced Yvette Mercier.

'*Taugenichts!*' cried Hilda Bhaer, at the other side of Kitty.

Such a noise and fuss as the middles made had rarely before been heard in the Chalet School, and it was only to be expected that someone should hear them and come to see what was the matter. This was Mademoiselle herself, and at first there was such a noise in the cloak-room that she could not hear herself speak. Finally, by dint of clapping her hands and shaking those nearest her, she got attention, and demanded in no uncertain tones to know the meaning of it all.

A silence followed her words. No one liked to tell tales; at the same time Mademoiselle was looking angrier than they had seen her for a long time, and obviously meant to get to the bottom of things.

55

However, Eustacia herself came to the rescue. 'I only boxed that rude child's ears,' she explained, pointing to the sobbing Kitty. 'She tried to knock me over, and then the others all laughed.'

'I didn't!' wept Kitty. 'I o-o-only g-got up, and b-bumped into h-h-her!'

'That is the truth, honour bright, Mademoiselle,' said Margia, who, since Eustacia had given herself away, saw no reason why she should remain silent. 'She banged into Eustacia and she was honestly beginning to say she was sorry. We laughed—it looked so awfully funny, And then Eustacia smacked her hard in the face—see!' And she drew down Kitty's hands from her face for Mademoiselle to examine it.

There, sure enough, were the prints of Eustacia's fingers, standing out in flaming red marks. Mademoiselle uttered a shocked exclamation, and then turned to Margia. 'You must take Kitty to Matron at once, Margia, and request her to bathe the place with something.—Ilonka, run across to Le Petit Chalet and ask Miss Wilson to call here for Kitty on her way out with the juniors.—Eustacia, fasten your scarf properly, and take your place in the line with Cornelia Flower.—And, remember, no one is to speak with Eustacia until I give permission.'

Chapter X

EUSTACIA MAKES MORE MISTAKES

IN deathly silence the ranks set out and marched steadily to the gate. The seniors led, followed by the senior and junior middles. Once they were beyond the Chalet grounds the girls were allowed to break ranks. The only restrictions were that they were not to stray, and must keep clear of trees. There was always danger from a rotten branch breaking beneath the weight of the snow, and Mademoiselle Lepâttre was careful.

It had frozen overnight, and the hard snow crunched crisply under the swift feet of the girls. On the still air their voices rang out clearly, and they enjoyed the brisk walk. Not all, however. Cornelia stuck to her post by Eustacia's side, wishing heartily that it had been given to someone else.

Presently Mademoiselle said, 'Cornelia, you have been very good. Eustacia will now walk with me, and you may run on and join the others.'

Cornelia needed no further bidding. She galloped off, and was presently to be seen with Evadne, Margia, Ilonka, Giovanna, Elsie, and others of the gang.

'Walk at my side, Eustacia,' said Mademoiselle gently.

Eustacia fell back obediently. There was something in the Head's voice that was irresistible. When they had been going a little way in silence, Mademoiselle broke the silence again. 'Why did you treat Kitty that way, my child?' she asked. 'It was unkind; it was unladylike. Your parents were gentle. What would they have thought of your action today?'

'You are all against me!' Eustacia burst out. 'You all try to make me unhappy. But you shall never do that!'

'No; it is yourself who make yourself unhappy,' said Mademoiselle quietly. 'Believe me, Eustacia, what we give to other people, that we may expect again. Now you have shown yourself to be in every way unlovable. Yet you complain because others do not love you.'

It was just what her aunt had said, but Eustacia was still too far wrapped up in herself to heed it. She stalked along beside Mademoiselle, her shoulders held stiffly, her expression one of sullen anger.

Mademoiselle turned her attention from the sulky girl at her side to the beauty all around them. They were going up a narrow valley now, walled in by the mountain-side. A fence cut off the pines that clad it from the path, and fence, path, and mountain-slopes were white with snow. Before them the valley widened to a tiny clearing, where stood a chalet on piles—a necessary precaution, since the stream which fed the Tiern See in spring and autumn was apt to flood when the thaws came. With its steep rock-anchored roof thick in snow, its blue-painted door and window-shutters, it looked like some fairy-tale house. Joey Bettany always declared that she expected to see the old witch from *Hansel and Gretel* come out of it some day. Evadne, who was *not* imaginative, had pointed out that they all knew the people who lived there—a woodman and his wife and two children; therefore, no witch was likely to make her appearance from the doorway—even supposing there *were* such things as witches!

With a wish to break up the heavy silence enveloping the girl beside her, Mademoiselle pointed out this charming little building, emphasising its fairy-like appearance.

'There are no such things as fairies,' said Eustacia coldly. 'I am not a baby to believe in such rubbish as that.'

'The greater pity!' reflected Mademoiselle.

At this point some of the Fourth came racing back to ask if they might call and inquire for the owners of the chalet. 'They won't have been able to get down to Briesau all last week, Mademoiselle,' urged Cornelia. 'Do let us!'

'And we have the doll for Gredel,' added Elsie Carr. 'You remember, she had a cold, and could not come to the Christmas tree at the end of term. We could tell them, and then the next time any of them are in Briesau they could call and get it.'

'Very well,' agreed Mademoiselle. 'Ask two of the prefects to go with you.'

The others were all waiting near, and as the sound of their merry voices broke across the stillness the door opened, and a stout woman, of the fair, peasant type, came out of the house. But the girls broke into horrified exclamations at sight of her face, and Joey, Marie, and Simone ran forward.

'Frau Steindal!' What is the matter?' demanded Joey in her fluent German.

At sight of them the woman burst into tears, and they thronged round her, trying to comfort her and to find out what was wrong. At length Mademoiselle, who, with her charge, had come up by this time, managed to make something of the broken flood of patois, and her kind plain face was overspread with a look of deep sympathy. She patted the sobbing woman on the shoulder, uttering words of consolation, and then bade the girls go forward, while Miss Annersley stayed behind to make some further inquiries.

'What's wrong?' asked Joey, when they were once more on their way.

'The little Gredel has never recovered from her cold, and all day she sits and coughs,' replied Mademoiselle. 'She grows thinner and thinner, and her breathing is bad. They fear—consumption.'

Joey's face became grave. 'That's bad,' she said. 'What can we do?'

'I will telephone to Dr. Jem, and ask that he or one of the others may come down as soon as possible to see the child,' replied the Head. 'Then, if he thinks it well, we will send her to the Sonnalpe. It may be in time yet, and the sanatorium never refuses a patient.'

'Oh, we'll manage that part all right,' agreed Joey. 'Poor little Gredel!'

'Tell the others who are here, but warn them to say nothing—but nothing at all—to the juniors,' continued Mademoiselle.

Jo went off to the others to tell them the sad news and to impress on them the fact that nothing was to be said before the juniors. The great sanatorium on the Sonnalpe was so closely connected with the school through Dr. Jem and Dr. Gottfried Mensch, as well as Dr. Maynard, brother of a former mistress, that its woes came very near them at times.

As Joey ran off, Mademoiselle turned to the girl beside her. 'And you, too, Eustacia. You will say nothing before the little ones.'

'I never talk to the children,' replied Eustacia indifferently. 'I am not likely to say anything to them.' However, before *Mittagessen*, when they were all in the common-room, she said something to Paula von Rothenfels for which the others didn't forgive her for a very long time. 'I think all this fuss about a mere peasant child is ridiculous. Even if they take her to the sanatorium and cure her, she will probably begin again, once she goes home again. These people know nothing about the laws of hygiene, and never dream of letting fresh air into their houses. Is it to be wondered at that the child should be suffering from tuberculosis?'

'You shut up!' said Evadne.

'You are extremely rude,' said Eustacia—it must be confessed, with a good deal of truth. 'I suppose you think you are clever, but that is a mistake. As for the child, she will probably die of the disease, and would most likely prefer to die among her own people. I cannot see any use in taking her from them.'

59

Joey happened to be standing near, and she promptly lost her temper. 'You perfect little beast!' she said furiously. 'How dare you talk like that, as if Gredel were a kitten or —or a pigling? It's a pity you weren't drowned when you were a baby! Then we shouldn't have had you here, with your beastly suggestions.'

It was quite indefensible, of course. Joey was a prefect, and her language was disgraceful. But most of those who heard it agreed with her, and even Mary Burnett made no attempt to rebuke her.

As for Eustacia, she laughed in Joey's furious face. 'Your own language and manners strike me as being on a par with those of the juniors,' she said. 'Really, it might have been as well for me to have gone to a council school in England as to come here, I think. I certainly could not have met with more hooliganism anywhere than in this wonderful Chalet School of yours.'

There was a silence on this, for the girls had all heard Joey's passionate words, and stopped talking to watch the march of events.

Now Mary came forward. 'That will do,' she said firmly. 'Go and sit down, all of you—Joey, Juliet was looking for you in the library. She wants some book or other, and you, as librarian, should know best where it is.'

At that reminder that she was a prefect, Joey shut her mouth with a snap, swung round, and stalked from the room, her black brows drawn in a scowl, her black eyes still flashing.

'The bell will go in a minute,' said Mary severely to the others. 'Get into your lines, please.—Eustacia, you are to go to Matron's room, and have your meals there for today. I was just coming to tell you. Will you please go there at once?'

Eustacia opened her lips to defy the head-girl, but something in Mary's calm gaze overawed her slightly, and she went with surprising meekness. As for the others, they took their places in silence because that was the rule; but they were all thinking hard enough, and many of them showed by their faces what their thoughts were.

Mary surveyed them all. 'You will say nothing to anyone about this,' she said abruptly. 'This is Sunday. Tomorrow we will call School Council and decide what we are to do about it all. There's the bell. Please lead on.'

Chapter XI

A HARD PROBLEM

FOR the rest of that day Eustacia found herself in isolation. Mademoiselle, coming to see her after *Mittagessen*, told her gently enough that her behaviour to Kitty had made it impossible for her to mingle with the others. Then she left her to Matron, who, having no inclination to gentleness of any kind, presented the indignant Eustacia with a prayer-book and desired her to learn and repeat from memory certain collects.

Eustacia had no lack of courage, but there was something in Matron's cold grey eyes that reduced her to a meek obedience that surprised herself when she thought it over that night. She learned the collects, repeated them correctly before *Kaffee und Kuchen*, which she took alone in Matron's room.

The next morning Mademoiselle announced judgment. Eustacia was to apologise to Kitty for having lost her temper, and for the next day she was to be isolated. That, it was hoped, would bring her to her senses.

So much for the decision of the staff. As for the scene which had taken place before *Mittagessen*, of that they had no knowledge, for Mary preferred to deal with it herself. She summoned the school to a meeting during break, and briefly told them exactly what had happened. 'We must try to make Eustacia realise that that sort of thing isn't done here,' she concluded. 'But I want to remind you all that she hasn't lived as we have. She's never been to school before, and never had any girl-friends.—Isn't that so, Joey?'

Joey nodded. 'She lived with her mother, who was a doctoress, and her father, who was a professor of some kind,' she said. 'They didn't let her have any friends but themselves. As Mary says, we must make allowances.'

'I don't see what allowances we can make for her smacking Kitty yesterday,' said Margia.

'That was done in a moment's temper,' said Deira.

'People often don't think when they lose their tempers—*I* know that!'

Mary glanced at her watch. 'Break is nearly over,' she said, 'and we have settled nothing. Will you all think about it, and let me know what you consider we ought to do? You can tell me during the day, and we meet again after *Kaffee und Kuchen* to decide finally. We can't have any girl in the Chalet School talking like a—a Bolshevist. And we're not going to allow any girl to slap another just when she sees fit. Only remember, there *are* allowances to be made, and *make* them. Oh, and by the way, I don't want any *silly* suggestions! This isn't a joke!'

Deira then got up. 'The Saints have challenged us to a snow-fight, to take place as soon as possible,' she announced. 'Are you all agreed to accept the challenge?'

'Three cheers!' shouted the irrepressible Evadne.

'That will do!' Mary interrupted her.

Evadne sat down again, and the School promptly called its desire to meet the girls of St. Scholastika's from the other side of the lake.

'Very well,' said Deira. 'I'll ask permission to ring up Gipsy Carson, and tell her that we'll meet them as soon as possible.' She paused, and looked at her fellow-prefects. 'Anything else, anyone? The bell's going in a minute.'

'Yes,' said Joey, leaping to her feet. '*I* have. I want contributions for the *Chaletian* as soon as you can let me have them. Last day for sending in, next Thursday.'

The bell rang for the end of break just then, and the meeting broke up. The girls streamed off to their form-rooms and work. The Fourth were to meet Miss Leslie, the new Maths mistress, who had taken the place of Miss Maynard, and who was to be there only until Juliet Carrick was through her course at the Royal Holloway. Then Juliet would come out to the Tiern See to become Maths mistress, and Miss Leslie, who was engaged to a young captain in the Indian army, was going home to be married. The girls liked what they had seen of her so far, and, finding her quick to detect any nonsense, but good fun out of school-hours, accorded her much the same respect they had given Miss Maynard.

On this morning, however, they were all stirred up over Eustacia and the coming snow-fight, and they had not been in the room ten minutes before Miss Leslie realised that she was facing a hard task. Algebra was not a favourite subject with the Fourth, which, as a whole, inclined rather to the literary side. This morning they all presented a highly excited demeanour, giggling and whispering, till the exasperated mistress could cheerfully have shaken every girl in the form. Eustacia was not there, since the isolation was to be complete. She was working in Mademoiselle's study by herself.

Presently Miss Leslie began to lose patience, and by the time that she had called the entire form to order three times; rebuked Cornelia sharply for trying to tie Suzanne Mercier's long plait to the back of her chair; threatened to send Elsie Carr into the corner if she continued to make faces at Evadne Lannis; and turned Ilonka Barkocz out of the room until she could control her giggles, she was thoroughly angry.

Finally, she swung round from the blackboard, where she had been demonstrating simple quadratics to them. 'Sit up, every one of you!' she commanded.

The Fourth sat up at once.

'Put everything out of your hands. No one is to have anything. Now fold your arms behind your backs. You can sit there for the rest of the lesson, in just that position, and don't let me have to complain of anyone fidgeting, please.— Cornelia, uncross your legs!'

Cornelia did as she was told, and set both feet firmly on the floor. The eyes of the Fourth went apprehensively to the clock. They had another twenty minutes to spend in this boring position. What was worse was Miss Leslie's detached attitude. She herself leaned back in her chair and let her gaze wander to the window, through which was to be seen the snowy garden, lovely in its robes of whiteness.

A movement from Evadne, who was a restless being and hated sitting still, brought the eyes of the mistress on her, and a sharp rebuke followed. 'I told you to sit still, Evadne. If you cannot do as you are told now, we will see what you can manage after *Mittagessen*. Understand, all of you, that if I have to speak again, I will see to it that you spend most of your free time for the rest of the week in this way.'

She obviously meant what she said, and the Fourth sat in grim stillness for the remainder of the time. They hated her during it, but when it was all over and she had taken her books and departed, after giving them an amount of preparation that made them gasp with horror, they acknowledged that she had won.

'She's no soft,' said Evadne. 'Guess we'd better pull up our socks for her for the future. I don't want any more of this!' She wriggled violently as she spoke.

'Neither do I,' agreed Ilonka. 'I have never sat so still before.'

'She's all there,' admitted Elsie Carr. 'I say! Here's Mademoiselle Lachenais! We'd better mind what we're doing. She may be feeling like Miss Leslie, too.'

But amiable little Mademoiselle Lachenais was in her most smiling mood, and they got through the rest of the morning without mishap. Then the bell rang for the end of school, and they were free to discuss their ideas for settling with Eustacia.

Many varied and wildly absurd suggestions were made. In two minutes, more than half the form was embroiled, and the main issue was lost.

They were brought to their senses by the arrival of Frieda Mensch, who had come up that morning, and who now marched in on them, asking if they were aware that the bell for *Mittagessen* had already rung twice. 'And see your hands and hair!' she finished.

The Fourth tore to the splasheries, and made frantic endeavours to reduce themselves to neatness in thirty seconds. A good many people came to table with hands and faces half-dried, and they were obliged to rub them surreptitiously with their handkerchiefs. It was well for them that the prefect on duty with them this week was Marie von Eschenau, who was notoriously easy-going, and who merely frowned at people who dived below the table suddenly for no apparent reason.

At the end of *Mittagessen* Mademoiselle rose in her seat. 'All the girls who were late will come to me for a punishment lesson when the others have left the room,' she said briefly.

The members of he Fourth looked at each other, and stifled groans. 'Punishment lessons' meant repetition—generally from some author they themselves dubbed 'boring'. They were right this time, for they were all set certain paragraphs from *Maria von Lichtenstein*, which had to be repeated before preparation that evening.

'German of all things!' groaned Evadne. 'I loathe the beastly crack-jawed language!'

'It was good enough for Goethe and Heine, so it is quite good enough for you,' said Joey, who had overheard her. 'Anyway, you asked for it—trailing in like that!'

She went on, and Evadne recovered from her fit of choking as best she might. Then they adjourned to the common-room, where rest was the order of the day, and dragged out their deck-chairs with many grumbles. This was the time when they might read story-books, but Evadne, who was certainly tempting Providence today, elected to bring her copy of *Maria von Lichtenstein*, and begin her punishment. Elsie, who sat near, leaned over, and the sinful pair had finished the first paragraph before the bell rang for the putting away of chairs. The others, who had not been so thoughtful, complained loudly, but Cornelia pointed out that it had been a risky thing to do. The prefect was Deira O'Hagan, and she might easily have taken it into her head to wander round and see what they were reading.

'Then I should have said that *Maria* was a story all right,' declared Evadne.

'Think she'd have believed you?' demanded Margia Stevens, who was present.

'She *might*!'

'She might *not*! Deira's not quite weak in the head.'

'Thank you,' observed Deira herself, as she passed them; and the pair were stricken dumb for the moment.

'Do you think she guessed?' demanded Evadne breathlessly, when she could speak.

Margia shook her head. 'No. She'd have come down on us like a cart-load of bricks if she had. She only heard what I said.'

At this point the school-bell rang, and they were obliged to separate. Margia went off to needlework, and Evadne marched to the common-room, where the Third and Fourth had singing together.

The Singing master, one Tristan Denny, was a queer-looking man, with flowing hair, bright eyes, and vivid pink-and-white skin. Music was his life, and if he had had his

C

own way, all lessons would have been based on music. He quoted what Plato had to say on the subject in season and out, and the girls had christened him 'Plato' in consequence. For all his idiosyncrasies, he was a fine teacher, and the School was famed for its singing.

For this lesson Eustacia was brought down to the class, and she faced the rather eccentric master somewhat contemptuously. He had not been able to teach the previous week, so this was the first time she had seen him. 'The man looks insane,' she thought to herself.

'Plato' handed Cornelia a bundle of songs and requested her to distribute them among the others. She did so, and found herself handing Eustacia one as politely as possible, though she *had* intended making a face at her. Eustacia looked at it. It was a setting of 'Abou Ben Adhem', by an English composer. She knew neither the words nor the music, but she liked the look of the words, and she was soon to discover that she also liked the music. It was modern, but with a wonderful flow and grace, and the girls, after humming it through at sight, soon showed a very good idea of it in the rough. Then came the detailed work, and Eustacia found that the singing lesson was by no means the baby's play she had expected. Nothing less than the best would do for Mr. Denny, and he had the gift of infecting his class with his own enthusiasm. Eustacia had never touched music in any shape or form, but hidden away in her was a real love for it, and this love was brought to light by the Singing master. Of them all, she revelled most in the delicate touches by which 'Plato' brought out the composer's meaning. Not even Cornelia, who possessed a charming voice, enjoyed it more than this strange child who was at odds with the whole world at present. It was a bitter grief to Eustacia when the lesson came to an end, and the forms marched out to their needlework class, while the Fifth and Sixth took their places. She went back to her exile in the study with one determination, to write home as soon as possible and ask if she might take music lessons.

Kaffee und Kuchen she had alone in Matron's room, and was then given a book and told to amuse herself till the prep-bell rang. For once, the book failed to hold her attention. Her mind was far away with music.

And meanwhile the School was facing the problem as to

what to do to make Eustacia Benson 'less like a savage', to quote Joey's expression.

Mary took the chair, and the other prefects sat round her in solemn phalanx. This was the most serious event of their careers as prefects so far, and on one had the faintest idea how to to deal with it. Mary rose to her feet when the last middle had sat down, called the meeting to order, and then asked for suggestions. 'I think we ought to consider the matter gravely,' she said. 'Please, will no one make silly suggestions, for it really is serious. Eustacia is hating us and the School very badly just now, and as long as she feels like this, she will not settle down. Also, we can't have her slapping people when she likes.'

A little silence followed, which was broken by Suzanne Mercier, who got up a little timidly to offer her idea of treating Eustacia kindly.

'We've done it up to now,' said Evadne, 'and a lot of use it's been!'

The meeting agreed with this dictum, so Suzanne sat down again, having accomplished nothing. Various other suggestions were put forward, but it was felt that none of them really met the situation.

Finally, Frieda Mensch had the best idea. 'Let us find out what it is she likes, and ask her to join the Hobbies Club,' she said. 'If she finds that we show real interest, it may make some difference.'

'I doubt it,' said Jo gloomily. 'Oh, we can try, of course; but Eustacia strikes me as the kind of girl who wouldn't have any hobbies.'

'We don't know that,' Mary pointed out. 'It's certainly the best of the lot. And you ought to speak to her about the *Chaletian,* Jo. She might like to give you an article.'

'What on?' demanded Jo, with more heat than good grammar. 'Maths? Or classics? I don't specially want an essay on the beauties of Sophocles or the wonders of Euclid, you know.'

'Still, you might try,' said Mary. 'What about asking her for a description of Oxford?'

'I should like that,' said Marie von Eschenau. 'I have much desire to see some day your great university town, Joey; and a description would be pleasant to read.'

'All right; I'll ask her. But I don't mind betting you she won't take it nicely,' said Jo.

Since nothing further could be suggested, the meeting ended there, and the members went off to prep, leaving the prefects to arrange how they should try to interest Eustacia in the Hobbies Club and the *Chaletian*, and being thankful that they had nothing to do with it.

Chapter XII

EUSTACIA AND THE OTHERS

'EUSTACIA—Eustacia! Wait a moment! I want to speak to you!'

Eustacia—released from solitiude—turned on her way down the corridor, to see Joey Bettany running after her.

'What do you want?' she asked coldly, as the prefect reached her. 'I am in rather a hurry.'

Joey swallowed her wrath at this off-hand manner, and proceeded to her point at once. 'Come into the library, will you? I want to show you our magazine—the *Chaletian*. We wondered if you would care to let us have an article on Oxford for it? What do you think?' She turned in at the door of the library as she spoke, and went over to a shelf, from which she took a slim, bound volume, which she held out to the younger girl.

Eustacia had made no attempt to follow her. Jo had made a bad mistake in bringing her to the library, for Eustacia had not forgiven the prefects for barring her from its pleasures, and the casual way in which Jo summoned her to it filled her with anger. 'Thank you, but you seem to have forgotten that you have forbidden me to enter,' she said.

Joey turned in surprise at her tone. 'That doesn't count when one of *us* brings you,' she declared.

'Does it not? Well, I see no reason why I should enter to please you, Josephine Bettany, and I prefer to stay outside,' said Eustacia.

'Why d'you try to keep on your own, Eustacia? Listen to me, and, for goodness sake, come in! I don't want the whole School to hear what I'm going to say!' She crossed the room as she spoke, and took the other girl's arm in a 'friendly grasp to draw her in.

But Eustacia wrenched her arm away, and turned on the startled Jo eyes glinting with rage. 'I refuse to be bullied like this!'

'Oh, my wig!' exclaimed Jo, now thoroughly exasperated. 'I *wasn't* bullying you, you——' She bit off the words on the end of her tongue, for she knew how Eustacia would resent being called a 'silly ass', and then went on more quietly. 'I didn't mean to hurt you, Eustacia, and I don't see how I could. Look here, if you won't come here, come on up to the prees' room, and then we can discuss this question of the article on Oxford in peace.'

'Thank you,' said Eustacia; 'but there is nothing to discuss.'

'But of course there is! I haven't told you the sort of thing I want, nor the length, nor anything.'

At this Eustacia's temper flamed out. 'And do you really think that you've only to ask to have?' she choked. 'I will *never* do you an article of any kind—NEVER!'

' "Never" is a pretty long time,' said Joey drily. 'All right; I see it's no use. Sorry I bothered you.' She turned her back on the other girl, and put the copy of the *Chaletian* back in its place on the shelf. Then she crossed over to a table, and began to clear up a litter of magazines.

Eustacia stood still in the doorway, watching her uneasily. She was not very sure what to do. She didn't like to go in case it savoured of running away. She had nothing further to say to Jo, who suddenly struck her as rather dignified. Therefore, she stood where she was.

Joey, busy with her work, paid no further heed to her until she had finished, and turned to leave the room. 'I think there is nothing more, thank you,' she said, as she reached the door. 'Do you wish to speak to me about anything else? No? Then, if you don't mind, I am going to lock the door. Excuse me.' She closed the door quietly behind her and locked it, and then went off, the key in her pocket.

Eustacia, having nothing else to do, turned and went to her own form-room. Unaccountably she found herself wishing that she had answered Jo differently. Though neither of them knew it at the time, a change had begun in Eustacia that very afternoon. Hitherto she had looked on all the girls as objectionable, lumping them all more or less together. Some had struck her as being worse than the others, but that was all. Now she felt a respect for Jo Bettany, who had controlled what Eustacia knew to be a hot temper, and answered her quietly instead of flaring out at her. The very circumstances of her early training had taught Eustacia to admire self-control, and though she refused to admit it to herself, secretly she admired the Chalet librarian, and of that admiration came, by slow degrees, a liking against which the younger girl fought hard, but which she was unable to conquer.

And Joey, strolling down the passage as if she had never a care in the world, told herself fiercely that never had she met a more disagreeable, unpleasant girl than Eustacia Benson. She went upstairs and reached the prefects' room, where Mary, Deira, Frieda, Simone, and Marie were all sitting. They looked up as she came in.

'Come and sit down, Joey,' said Mary, pulling a chair round beside her own. 'Have you much for the *Chaletian*?'

'*Blow the Chaletian!*' returned Jo, perching herself on the broad window-sill and looking gloomily up the valley.

The others exchanged glances. They knew now, as well as if Joey had told them, that she had seen Eustacia on the subject of the article and had been rudely repulsed. With a warning frown at the others, Mary stretched out her hand and took a box off the table. 'Toffee for me this morning,' she said. 'Catch, Joey.'

Joey caught the tin which was tossed to her and abstracted a piece, her face relaxing a little.

'What about this snow-fight with the Saints?' asked Frieda. 'I have heard that there is to be one, but that is all I know. May I have the details, someone?'

'It takes place tomorrow—if the weather is fit,' said Mary. 'We are having it on the water-meadows at two o'clock. We fight for an hour, and then all come here for *Kaffee*. I rather think they are fixing up a return match next week. The snow came so early, it may go early this spring, so it's best to have these things while there's no danger of a thaw.'

'As we are still in January——' began Jo.

'Oh, I know!' Mary interrupted her. 'But the end of next week is February, and February is a short month. Besides, half-term comes then. We have the sale at the end of the term, and we must work once half-term is over. It's a good thing the Saints are coming in, isn't it?'

'Very good,' said Frieda. 'And will Juliet be here then?'

'For half-term—or the sale, d'you mean? I haven't an idea. I shouldn't think so, though.'

'She's going back the week after next,' said Joey, condescending to leave her splendid isolation by the window and stroll over to the others. 'I had a note from my sister this morning, and she says Dr. Jem tells her Juliet is quite fit again, and she doesn't want to lose more time than she can help. As it is, she'll have to work jolly hard to make up for this. She's only waiting to see Bernie again.'

'They come back next week,' said Frieda, with a sigh. 'It will be lonely at home, with Gottfried and Bernhilda both away.'

'But you'll be all coming here for the summer,' Jo reminded her consolingly. 'Onkel Reise said so on Saturday when he was up. Gottfried and Gisela will be quite near then.'

Frieda brightened up. 'Yes, that is true.'

At this moment there came the sound of flying feet down the corridor, and then Evadne Lannis and Paula von Rothenfels tumbled into the room, their eyes wide with horror.

'Oh, Mary!' gasped Paula, speaking her own language in the excitement of the moment. 'You must come at once!'

'Sooner!' shrieked Evadne.

Mary caught the pair by the shoulders and gave them a slight shake. 'What has happened?' she demanded.

'Eustacia went into the chemmy lab, an' she's upset that big bottle of something-or-other acid all over the floor!'

Mary gasped. 'Come along, all of you! She *can* only mean the hydrochloric, and I don't suppose there'll be any floor left at that rate!—Evvy! Go and get Bill, and tell her what's happened!—Oh! When I get hold of Eustacia——'

She tore out of the room, followed by the others, and they all raced down the stairs at such a pace that they brought those of the staff who were in the house out of their room and the staff-room to find out what was the matter. Mademoiselle was out, and Matron had two feverish colds in the sick-room, so they put in no appearance. But the rest were there and were soon on the spot, where a bevy of middles were all standing at the door of

71

the chemistry laboratory, exclaiming in horror, while Eustacia, white and frightened, stood in a corner with Suzanne and Ilonka.

Miss Annersley, who had been in the staff-room, was on the spot almost as soon as the prefects, and promptly demanded the reason for all this. She was answered by half-a-dozen people, who forgot rules, and spoke in their own tongues.

'Silence!' she cried at length.—'Mary, what is that on the floor?'

'Hydrochloric acid—I *think*,' faltered Mary.

'Hydrochloric! Good heavens! The floor will be eaten away! Where is Miss Wilson?'

'Evadne has gone to fetch her,' said Jo, who was regarding the scene with deep interest. 'I say, oughtn't we to get something to neutralise it? Anyone know what we can use?'

Before anyone could answer, Miss Wilson burst through the throng her hair all tossed by her wild race from Le Petit Chalet, and looked at the mess. For a moment she said nothing, then she heaved a deep sigh. 'Thank goodness! It was nothing but the distilled water! I *thought* I had locked the hydrochloric away!'

'Are you *sure*?' asked Miss Annersley.

'Positive! But I'll look in the cupboard to be certain.' She produced her keys, and unlocked the great cupboard where all the dangerous acids and alkalis were kept. There, sure enough, was the great bottle of hydrochloric, safe and sound. The Science mistress relocked the door, and then turned to the sink for a swab. With this she swabbed up the mess, picking up the bottle, which lay on its side, and setting it on one of the benches.

The rest watched her with breathless interest, and when she had finished, and wrung out her swab, Evadne was, characteristically, the first to break the silence. 'Praise the pigs!' she said aloud.

Like a flash, 'Bill' was on her. 'Quite so! And now, do you mind explaining what you children were doing here at all? And how, pray, did you get in? I locked it up when I left this evening, I know.'

There was silence again. Everyone looked at everyone else, and no one spoke. Then Mary stepped forward.

'Evadne came for us, Miss Wilson,' she said. 'She told us that there had been an accident, and we all came.'

'Except me,' put in Evadne. 'Mary sent me flying for *you*, Miss Wilson.'

'I am glad she had the sense,' replied Miss Wilson. 'However, it was only what I might have expected from her. But that does not explain how *you* got into the laboratory, Evadne.'

Evadne blushed, and scrubbed her right foot up and down her left leg. 'I—I—saw the door—open, and I—just —came,' she faltered at length.

'And the rest of you?'

'We heard a yell, and came to see what was happening,' explained Elsie Carr.

Miss Wilson pulled out some stools, and signed to the mistresses present to sit down. 'Now, I want to get to the bottom of this,' she said severely. 'Which girl opened the door in the first instance?—Evadne, was it you?—Paula— Elsie—Cornelia——'

'It was I,' said a badly frightened voice.

Miss Wilson turned round 'Eustacia!' she exclaimed. '*You!* But you don't do science!'

With all eyes on her, Eustacia blushed crimson. 'No,' she said. 'I only wanted somewhere to read in peace.'

'Well—upon—my—word!' said Miss Wilson. She looked helplessly at the rest of the staff. 'Did you hear *that*?' Then she turned to the hapless Eustacia again. 'And how did you get in?'

'I took the key from the staff-room,' said Eustacia, who, whatever her faults, did not lack courage.

'Seems to make a habit of it,' murmured Joey at this point; but Mary trod so heavily on her foot that she barely suppressed a squawk of anguish, and Miss Annersley, catching the expression on her face, said sternly, 'Josephine! Kindly stop pulling faces!' Then she turned to the other mistresses.—'I think we don't need all these children. They had better go back to whatever they were doing. And Eustacia had better come to the staff-room. It will be warmer there.'

Miss Wilson nodded, and got up. The senior-mistress dismissed the other girls, and then, with Miss Wilson, marched Eustacia to the staff-room. Arrived there, the two mistresses held a brief but thorough inquisition, the upshot

73

of which was that Eustacia confessed that she had gone into the staff-room and, finding no one there to ask, had taken down the key of the chemistry laboratory, and had gone there to read. In settling down at a bench, she had accidentally pushed over the great jar containing the distilled water, and the crash, together with her own horrified scream, had startled Evadne and attracted Paula. Evadne, seeing the jar, had at once leapt to the conclusion that it was the hydrochloric acid which had gone, and had flown to bring the prefects, after shrieking to Eustacia not to touch the mess unless she wanted the skin taken off her hands. Not knowing what to do, the new girl had obeyed her, and, in the meantime, the other middles, aroused by Evadne's shouts and flight, had come trooping along to see what it all meant. Arrived there, they too had thought it to be hydrochloric acid that was meandering over the floor, and had repeated Evadne's warning to Eustacia not to touch it.

Eustacia brought her recital to a close, and then stood looking at the two mistresses.

'But how dared you take my keys like that?' asked Miss Wilson, when she had recovered her breath. 'How dared you have the impertinence to do such a thing?'

'I wanted somewhere to read in peace,' explained Eustacia, as though that accounted for everything.

'You must be mad!' declared the Science mistress hotly. 'How you had the impudence to do such a thing, I cannot imagine!'

'I did not mean it for impudence,' said Eustacia.

Miss Wilson found nothing to say to *that*. She merely looked helplessly at Miss Annersley, who took up the tale.

'But, Eustacia, you *must* have known that it was a very wrong thing for you to take that key without permission. In this school, rooms, when they are locked, are locked for a purpose. Apart from that, it is the rule that no girl goes into either of the laboratories unless the Science mistress is there with her. We have no wish for any accident to happen. You have been flagrantly disobedient, and, I am afraid, underhand.'

'I was *not* underhand,' said Eustacia angrily. 'I told you about the key at once.'

'Not exactly at once,' said Miss Wilson drily. 'I had begun inquiries before you saw fit to own up.'

Eustacia set her lips in rigid lines and a sullen expression came over her face. 'I didn't mean any harm,' she muttered.

'That is not the point,' said Miss Wilson, who was justifiably angry. 'At present we are concerned with the facts that you steal my keys and break one of the strictest rules of the School. If that bottle had contained hydrochloric acid, it would have meant that a good part of the flooring of the lab would have had to be renewed. You might even have burnt yourself severely, and *we* should have been blamed. You might easily have gained the School a bad name for carlessness. And all you have to say in the way of apology is that you "meant no harm"! *Do* you consider that an adequate expression of regret?'

'I wanted somewhere to read,' reiterated Eustacia.

'But, Eustacia,' expostulated Miss Annersley, 'can you not see that you have been very wrong? If this goes on, I do not see how we can be expected to keep you here. You do not wish to be sent away in disgrace, do you? It would mean that you would be regarded as a girl whom we could not trust—who had not sufficient sense of honour for us to trust you. That would be a bad beginning indeed to your life.'

Eustacia's head went down. The tears were pricking at the backs of her eyes, but she would almost rather have died than let the two mistresses know that. She bit her lips, and managed to keep back the sobs that were rising in her throat.

Miss Annersley, looking keenly at her, guessed what she was feeling, and decided to end the interview. She rose from her seat. 'I cannot decide about your punishinment tonight, Eustacia. Mademoiselle must see to that. For the present, I think you had better go to bed, and then, at least, we shall know where you are and what you are doing. Will you go and tell Matron that I want her here, and then go to bed at once? Mademoiselle will not return till late, and, therefore, cannot see you till the morning. And do, my dear girl, consider that you are one of a community now, and must abide by the rules of that community.'

Eustacia turned on her heel and left the room. She managed to gain control over herself, and gave Miss Annersley's message to Matron in steady tones. Then she retired to bed with all speed, and, curled down under the plumeau—Matron had stitched her blankets to it, so there was no further question of her discarding it at nights—she cried wretchedly till her handkerchief was sopping wet, and her pillow damp, and she fell asleep from sheer weariness.

Matron, coming up later with her supper, found her slumbering soundly, her lashes still wet, and the marks of the tears on her cheeks. The domestic tyrant of the School set down her tray, and drew the clothes closer round Eustacia with a softer expression than most people had seen on her face. 'Poor little soul!' she murmured pitifully. 'Poor, untrained little soul!'

Chapter XIII

NEXT DAY

EUSTACIA was interviewed by Mademoiselle next day, and after a long talk with her, the Head of the School forbade her going into either of the laboratories; made her give her word of honour that she would never again abstract keys which did not belong to her; set her ten French fables to learn by heart, and made an end of the matter.

'She must be quite mad,' said Joey, referring to Eustacia, when the prefects were discussing the matter next day. 'I thought it was cheek enough when she bagged my key; but to take the staff's——' She stopped short, evidently feeling that words were inadequate at this juncture.

'*I* don't see what we are to do with her,' said Mary helplessly. 'Oh, *what* a term we are having!'

'I warned you not to talk too soon,' returned Jo. 'All the same,' she added, 'I never thought of anything like this happening.'

'Nor could anyone else,' said Frieda, who was with them. 'Well, we had best get ready for the snow-fight, had we not? Does Eustacia play, also?'

'I suppose so.' Mary sounded weary. 'For goodness' sake, keep an eye on her, Frieda, and see that she doesn't do anything silly!'

'If you ask me, I should say that she's a great deal more likely to disapprove of the whole affair, and refuse to have anything to do with it,' said Jo. 'D'you think she ever *was* young?'

'Shouldn't think so. I should have said she was born grown-up,' returned Mary, getting up from her seat.

They followed her downstairs and into the cloak-rooms, where they changed into outdoor garb, putting on thick climbing-breeches, nailed boots, and heavy sweaters, with scarves tied crosswise over their chests. Fingerless mittens, and tam-o'-shanters completed their dress, and then they were ready. They left the place, and went off to see that the middles were prepared, and Jo straightway became embroiled in an argument with Eustacia, who declined to put on her breeches.

'They are most unladylike garments,' declared the younger girl.

Joey suppressed a grin, and settled down to persuade her. 'Really, Eustacia, they are all right. Everyone wears them for climbing. You see, they are so much safer than skirts. And they are very warm—that is why we are going to wear them this afternoon. Do put them on, and hurry up! You are keeping everyone waiting.'

'I will not wear such unmaidenly things,' said Eustacia stiffly.

Not for the first time, Jo longed to shake her soundly. However, she kept her head, and held out the abhorred garments. 'Really, Eustacia, you had better put them on. If you don't, I shall be obliged to report to whoever's on duty, and I don't want to do that. *Do* get into them, an' buck up!'

'I refuse,' said Estacia. 'You may tell all the tales you like, but that cannot make me put on such things.'

Joey laid them down and retired to seek the mistress on duty. It was Miss Wilson, and she, after listening to what the prefect had to say, sent for Matron, and requested her to see that the rebel was ready in ten minutes. 'Or I'll give you a quarter of an hour,' she added. 'Hurry her up, Matron; there's a dear!'

Matron went off with a grim face and a manner that permitted of no argument. In the cloak-room she merely picked up the breeches and held them out to Eustacia. 'Now then, put these on and hurry up. I have no time to stand here arguing with you! If you don't get into them in five minutes' time, I shall treat you as though you were the Robin, and put you into them myself.'

Matron was not big, but she was very wiry and muscular, and would have been perfectly capable of doing as she said. Also she possessed an eye that had never yet failed in its quelling powers. Eustacia found herself meekly donning the despised garments, and, what is more, doing so with all speed. In exactly twelve minutes' time Matron brought her to Miss Wilson ready for the fray.

Miss Wilson marched her off to join the others outside. Once she was out in the open air, Eustacia began to forget how miserable she was.

They reached the battle-ground, to find it already occupied by the girls of St. Scholastika, many of whom came forward with eager greetings. There had been a time when the two schools had been at daggers drawn, but that was now at an end.

The mistresses arranged that the juniors should have their own battle in a corner away from the others. The elder girls would not mean to be rough, but they might be so unintentionally, and no one wanted an accident.

The Chaletians occupied a kind of natural fort, made by the burying of some low bushes under the snow. Mary was their leader, with Deira and Jo as her seconds. Frieda had charge of the ammunition-making, three of the smallest middles being her lieutenants. To Marie and Simone was entrusted the defence of the back of the fort, and some of the older middles under Paula von Rothenfels were to see to the keeping up of the fort.

The 'Saints', under Gipsy Carson, divided their army into three parts. The left wing, under Hilda Wilmot, was to try to get round to the back of the fort, and storm it. The right wing was to be led by Doris Potts, a tall sturdy girl, who was good at all sports, and was to 'make' for the side; the centre, under Gipsy herself, would attack from the front. Certain girls from each division were detailed to provide the others with ammunition, and were left to the care of Maisie Gomm, who never could be trusted to keep her head in any excitement, and might, as Gipsy said, 'do any daft thing that struck her'.

Then the two armies retired to their places; there was a pause, to give everyone time to make snowballs; Miss Wilson's whistle rang out, and the battle began.

Gipsy led her men forward at a rush, while the wings broke away and made for their appointed places. In the fort, Mary warned her girls to save their balls till the enemy were close at hand. Then the balls were all flung rapidly. Under the withering fire the 'Saints' drew back for a moment; but Maisie and her followers came running up with fresh ammunition, and the attackers rallied once more and advanced. Those in the fort found it would take them all their time to keep the enemy out, and were hard at it. Even Eustacia became infected by the general excitement, and made balls as fast as she could, though at first she had been inclined to sneer at this 'babyish' game. At the back, Hilda Wilmot and her satellites were attacking hard, and Winnie Silksworth even managed to break through the wall, but she was grabbed by Bianca di Ferrara and dragged in shrieking at the full pitch of her lungs, the first prisoner to be taken by either side. She was then sent over to help with the little ones, for it had been arranged that any girl taken captive was to be out of it altogether.

Before long there were others to join her, for Joy Bettany made a sortie against Doris Potts's men and found she was not strong enough. Screaming wildly they made for the fort again; and though most of them got back in time, Cyrilla Maurús and Suzanne Mercier were captured by Doris, and so were out of it, much to their disgust.

Paula and her lieutenants discovered that they had all they could do to keep the walls of the fort anything like standing, and had it not been for the bushes there would have been none. Those same bushes were of great help to the defenders, for more than one of the enemy got entangled with them, and so were taken prisoner.

Back and forth flew the balls, and everyone was soon well powdered with the feathery snow, which clung like fine powder to their clothes but, since it was so dry, did no one any harm. The staff kept an eye on the girls, ready to withdraw any who might tire easily, and to see that no one came to any other harm. Joey Bettany and Hilda Wilmot were called off half-way through, much to their own disgust. But neither was strong and Joey had come through a serious illness during the previous term, and had to be watched for signs of over-fatigue. They were set to walking about to keep them warm, and presently Miss Wilson sent them on to the Chalet to say that the battle would end in another twenty minutes, and would Matron please see that *Kaffee und Kuchen* were ready. With them went a few more people who had been looking tired out, and they raced home in fine style. There they shed their outer garments, and then ran to the *Speisesaal* to see what they could do to help with *Kaffee*.

Presently they heard gay voices, and then the two armies came into sight, all very rosy, all very breathless, and all, even Eustacia, very untidy.

'Well? Who won?' shrieked Jo, as Elaine, Mary, and Gipsy came into sight.

'Dead heat,' called Mary. 'Prisoners were equal, and, except for the bushes, there weren't any walls left to the fort.'

'Oh, good! Come along, you people. *Kaffee's* ready. Trot off to the cloakers and splasheries. Bell will go in ten minutes.'

They trooped off to make themselves tidy. It was a very merry business, for there were thirty more girls than were normally there, and the cloak-room accommodation was stretched to its utmost limits. At length all were ready, and they entered the *Speisesaal*, where *Kaffee* was steaming from the cups, and everyone fell to with an appetite that showed how strenuous had been their task.

Seated at her own table, Jo glanced across at Mary's, and her lips suddenly fell apart. Near the foot was seated Eustacia, between two of the 'Saints'. There had been such a crush that she had not had much time to make herself tidy, and had, perforce, to let her hair go. The hard work of the afternoon had ruffled and loosened it, and now it rippled round her face with a pretty, natural wave. The difference made to her by that loosening of her hair was marvellous, and it was added to by the flush brought by exercise and excitement to her usually pale face. For once she had forgotten all her grievances, and was talking and laughing almost as naturally as any of them.

'I *do* believe,' said Jo to herself, as she hospitably pressed cake on Winnie Silksworth—'I *do* believe that Eustacia has it in her to be downright pretty! And she looks even as though she might be jolly if you could only get her opened out! She's not like the same girl!'

And, indeed, she was not. Though she couldn't have explained it to herself, Eustacia felt almost as though a spell had been laid on her. For the first time it struck her that the girls amongst whom she found herself were very willing to be friendly.

The sale which was to come at the end of term was also discussed, and the free wards at the sanatorium came in for consideration. The 'Saints' were now filled with a desire to have their own cot in the children's ward, as the Chalet School had, and were working hard to get the money for it. Eustacia heard them talking about it, and also listened to one or two stories that made her think. She might have known all this sooner, but she had refused to listen. Now she listened with all her ears, and thought hard, if she said little. That was a long and jolly meal, and the big urns of milky coffee were emptied by the time everyone had had as much as she wanted. Then Miss Soames smilingly arose and thanked the Chalet School for its hospitality, and gave an invitation to all present to come to St. Scholastika's after the return match, which, they hoped, would take place in eight days' time.

It was accepted rapturously. Then the 'Saints' got into their outdoor things again, with many groans for stiffening muscles, and, with many 'Good-byes', set off under the starry skies to walk round the lake to Buchau, where St. Scholastika's stood.

'Preparation for one hour, *mes petites*,' said Mademoiselle, when the door had been shut and they were all in the common-rooms. 'After that, hot baths and bed for everyone, or you may be very stiff tomorrow."

They streamed off to preparation, and Eustacia never realised that she had not touched her hair since she had come in. Thus it hung loosely for the rest of the evening, and she was startled and gratified by heedless Kitty Burnett's remark, 'Why, Eustacia, I didn't know you could look so pretty!'

Chapter XIV

MADGE PAYS A VISIT

IT was a pity that the good feeling that had been established
during the snow-fight could not continue. However, human
nature being what it was, nothing was less likely, and before
twenty-four hours had passed Eustacia was again embroiled
with her school-fellows. This time it was the Fifth. Margia
Stevens was the victim, but the whole form took up her
cause with enthusiasm, and there was soon a very pretty
split between them and the Fourth. It began with Eustacia's
fountain-pen. This was a very excellent one, of which the
young lady was extremely proud. Careful and neat in most
things, she rarely left her pen anywhere. On the day following the great battle, however, for some reason she left it on
Margia's desk in the Fifth-form room, where the Fourth
had been having French.

Margia, coming to preparation after Singing, found the
pen, and promptly held it up. '*Someone* is jolly careless!'
she declared. 'Just see what one of the Fourth has left on
my desk. What shall we do with it? Lost property, I
suppose!'

'It's Eustacia's,' said Bianca di Ferrara, after looking at
it. 'I have heard about it. *We* have not such pens here.'

'Nor anywhere else,' laughed Louise Redfield, an American girl who had come that term.

Pretty Anne Seymour held out her hand for it, and
examined it carefully. 'Gold bands and everything,' she
said. 'It's much too good for a Fourthite!'

'Well, she ought to be more careful,' decided Margia.
'And we can't put a thing like that in L.P. It might slip
down somewhere and get lost. I'll take it to Charlie.'

'Charlie', it should be explained, was Miss Stewart, the
full name being 'Bonnie Prince Charlie'. Jo Bettany had
originated it, and it had caught on with the whole School.
Miss Stewart was as much a favourite as any of the staff,
being young, pretty, cheerful, and possessed of a great sense

of humour. She and Miss Wilson were great friends and, now that Miss Maynard, the last of the old staff, had gone, they were, perhaps, the most popular of all the mistresses, Mademoiselle alone excepted.

But Miss Stewart had one idiosyncracy. She detested carelessness about one's personal belongings, and was apt to deal sharply with any she met. If Margia were to hand the pen over to her, Eustacia was likely to receive a sharp scolding. The rest of the Fifth, knowing Margia, knew also that it was a joke on her part, and laughed at the threat. Unfortunately 'Charlie' herself came in in time to catch them, and at once demanded the cause of the laughter. Nobody liked to enlighten her, so they all sat still, while Margia hid the pen among her books and looked seraphic. Normally, it would have been all right; but 'Charlie' had been suffering tortures all night and all that day from a tooth that needed stopping, and her face was already slightly swollen. She promptly leapt to the conclusion that it was her lopsided appearance at which the girls were laughing, and, pain having sent her sense of humour adrift for the time being, she became insistent. 'I must know, girls. Please do not let me have to speak again!'

With Miss Stewart talking and looking like that, there was nothing for it but to tell her—or, at least, to tell her as little as they could, and trust to luck that she would not inquire too closely. Therefore Margia rose to her feet and reluctantly confessed that it was something she had said.

'What was it?' demanded the mistress sharply.

'A-about another girl,' stammered Margia.

'Which other girl? It is no use your prevaricating, Margia. I intend to get to the bottom of this, so the sooner you tell me everything the better for the whole form, for I shall keep you here until I know.'

'It was Eustacia,' admitted Margia.

'And what were you saying about her?'

Margia looked wildly around for inspiration. Finding none anywhere, she had, perforce, to meet Miss Stewarts' angry eyes again. There was no doubt about it, 'Charlie' meant what she had said. Margia felt that she had done her best to save any trouble, but trouble was not to be averted it seemed. Therefore she drawled as reluctantly as possible, 'She had left something on my desk—at least, we *think* it must be hers.'

'You aren't sure? What was it?'

Margia cast an imploring glance at the mistress, but it was wasted, for 'Charlie' merely held out her hand, repeating, 'What was it?'

Seeing no other help for it, the Fifth former produced the pen, and laid it in that outstretched hand. 'Charlie's' face darkened. Only that morning she had had cause to lecture Evadne Lannis for leaving her fountain-pen lying about. It was a strange week in which one of the Fourth was *not* in trouble for that very thing. Scarcely a lesson went by that someone didn't say, 'I've lost my fountain-pen, Miss Stewart', and lessons were hindered thereby. Eustacia was the final straw.

Now, with the pain in her face nagging furiously and worn out with a sleepless night, Miss Stewart was wrathful, and made up her mind to make an example of Eustacia and so teach the entire form a lesson, in the hope of putting an end to this tiresome carelessness. 'Very well,' she said coldly, opening her attaché-case and dropping the pen therein. 'I am sorry you saw fit to take such a long time over answering me, Margia. You may all lose an order mark for not doing your work properly, and Margia may learn Milton's sonnet on the massacre of the Piedmontese, and repeat it to me before *Frühstück* tomorrow morning.'

This was an unpleasant punishment, especially for Margia, who hated Milton and all his works from the depths of her heart. The Fifth went on with their work quietly—she told them to do so. But there was hatred in their hearts, and it is doubtful if they profited much by their energies for the rest of the afternoon.

Singing was the last lesson the Fourth and Third had that afternoon, and when it was over they returned to their form-rooms to put away their books before going upstairs to change for *Kaffee und Kuchen*. Eustacia soon discovered her pen to be missing, and turned out her locker at once.

'What's up?' asked Evadne, seeing her at work.

For once, Eustacia did not reprove her for slang, but instead said simply, 'I have lost my fountain-pen.'

'I say! That's hard luck!' Evadne was all sympathy. 'Did you have it in prep?'

'Yes,' said Eustacia.

'Did you not perhaps leave it in the Fifth-form room?' suggested Ilonka.

'I do not think so. I am not usually careless,' said Eustacia.

'Still, we had rather a scrum to clear out before the Fifths came, you remember,' said Elsie, joining in the discussion. 'I should go and ask, if I were you.'

'I'll come with you, shall I?' asked Evadne, slipping a hand through the other girl's arm, and, wonder of wonders, Eustacia did not shake her off.

Together they went to the Fifth-form room, and Margia knew what they wanted as soon as she saw them. Being Margia, she plunged headlong into it, and not too tactfully either. 'You've come about your pen, Eustacia,' she began. 'Well, I'm awfully sorry, but Charlie has it.'

'Charlie has it?' cried Evadne, before Eustacia could say a word. 'Oh, I say! You weren't such a mean as to give it to her, were you?'

'Of course I wasn't!' She found out about it, and took it!' snapped Margia, up in arms at once at the bare suggestion of meanness.

'I must go and ask for it,' said Eustacia. 'I am glad it is safe, for I feared I had lost it. Will you come with me, Evadne?' It was a great concession on her part, but she was still feeling the influence of that spell laid on her the previous day—hence the invitation.

'I say! You can't just go to Charlie like that,' said Anne Seymour quickly. 'She seemed to be awfully mad about it; and if I were you, Eustacia, I'd keep clear of her till she's cooled down a bit. If you go now, she'll probably just confiscate it, and read you a sermon a mile long on carelessness!'

'That's true,' said Margia ruefully. 'I'm fearfully sorry, Eustacia. I know it was mostly my fault——'

'Nonsense!' broke in Bianca. 'The first fault was with Eustacia, who left her pen on your desk, and no one can say that you did not do your best to keep it from Charlie.'

'But—I don't understand,' cried Eustacia. 'How should any mistress keep my pen?'

'Charlie is mad about something—toothache, probably,' said Anne wisely. 'Her face is all swollen at one side. We were laughing about the pen when she came in to take prep, and she insisted on knowing what it was. Margia did her best, but she simply *glued* to her till she knew all about it. Then she took the pen and slanged us all round, and gave us all order marks, and Margia rep. She really is in a hectic mood, and I wouldn't go to her just yet.'

'But this is injustice!' cried Eustacia. 'I have never left anything before, and to punish me because you were laughing is not fair!'

'She isn't—but for leaving your pen about,' said Margia.

'Why must you laugh over it?' Eustacia was losing her temper. 'Why could you not have put it away quietly and given it to me later? But I suppose it was to get me into trouble!'

'I think you might have put it away, as Eustacia says,' put in Evadne thoughtlessly. 'It wasn't like you, Margie!'

At this, Margia lost *her* temper and flared out, 'I didn't try to make her see it! She just *saw* it!'

'Couldn't you have sat on it?' asked Evadne.

'No, I couldn't! You know what Charlie is! And she's as mad as a hatter this afternoon! I'm sorry if it gets Eustacia into a row, but it can't be any worse than the one I'm in! And that *beastly* Milton to learn, too!' enlarged Margia, with little heed to rules about slang.

'Well, I suppose it cannot be helped,' said Eustacia coldly. 'I feel sure you did what you *could*, Margia.—Shall we go, Evadne?' Followed by Evadne, she left the room, and made her way to the staff-room—whither Evadne did *not* follow.

Instead, the little American dashed back to the common-room, murmuring, '*Oh!* Isn't Eustacia the born *edge*!'

In the staff-room Eustacia got short-shrift from Miss Stewart, whose face seemed to be all ache and whose every nerve was on the stretch. She gave way to temper, and Eustacia was left gasping and breathless after the History mistress had finished with her. She left the staff-room almost dazedly, realising that she would not get back her pen till half-term, and that Miss Stewart had the poorest opinion of her tidiness.

By the time she had reached the common-room Eustacia had recovered slightly, and was grasping the fact that, had it not been for Margia, this need not have happened.

On the spur of the moment, she rushed off to the senior-common-room, routed out Margia, who was in the throes of memorising that hateful sonnet, and poured out on her the vials of wrath which had boiled over in her.

Margia, irritated and impatient, and not possessed of too

good a temper herself, was not slow in retorting, and soon they were having a pitched battle of it. Marton arrived in the middle of things, and ordered them both off to bed at once. She also gave them her unbiased opinion of them. The Fourth, for once, took Eustacia's side, and there was soon a pretty little feud between the two forms, for the Fifth, naturally, took up the cudgels for Margia.

On to all this there came a little oil of peace when Mademoiselle announced one morning at *Frühstück* that Mrs. Russell was coming down that day for a day or two if the weather held. She wanted to see to one or two business matters, and, since she would be unable to have Joey and the Robin with her for half-term as usual, wished to see something of them now.

'What!' protested Joey. 'Not go to the Sonnalpe at half-term? But why?'

'Madame will tell you when she sees you,' replied Mademoiselle.

Mrs. Russell arrived late in the afternoon, and explained to the pair what had happened. 'I told you that I could not get down for March, and I told you why,' she began, when they were all comfortably established—Madge in a big chair with the Robin on her knee; Jo curled up on a low stool at her feet.

'I know,' said Joey. 'Jem's having those old doctors to stay to see the result of the new treatment. You've got to be there to look after them, I know. But what's it got to do with us not coming up at half?'

'We shall need every room in the place,' explained her sister. 'This is likely to be a big thing if its comes off, and doctors are coming from most of the important places. As you know, the hotel only holds a limited number, and though some of the people are coming down here for the time being, there are some we cannot ask to leave.'

Joey nodded. She knew what her sister meant. These were the folk who had in the big sanatorium relatives so seriously ill that their own rooms must be close at hand if it were humanly possible.

'That,' went on Madge, 'means that all of us there must take in as many of the visitors as possible. Jem and I have one of the biggest chalets. We are asked to entertain seven of the most famous specialists in this thing, and we can only do that by giving up every room possible. Even the little dressing-room which Robin has when she comes will be used—Papa, Robinette, is giving up his room, and is going to sleep there for the month.'

'Goodness!' exclaimed Joey.

'So, you see, we shall want every room we have, and we cannot have you this time. I'm very sorry, but it cannot be helped. Still, I have done what I could to make this a happy half-term for you, and I have arranged for you to go to Fulpmes, at the foot of the Stubai glacier. If the weather is fit, you may be able to go up to see the glacier itself, and that will be something new for both of you. There is only one thing about it—and I wish I had been able to arrange things differently—that will not be quite as you would like it, I am afraid. And that is that some of the others must be with you. Miss Wilson and Miss Stewart will be in charge of the English and American girls, and they have agreed to have you in their party. The Italian girls are going to the Schwarzwald with Miss Nalder and Miss Annersley; and the others go to Salzburg with Mademoiselle Lachenais. But you will be all of one nationality, and it will be a rather longer exeat than usual, for you are finishing on Thursday afternoon and not returning till Tuesday night.'

'But—the English and American girls,' said Jo. 'Who will that be?'

'Well, not Mary nor her sisters, for they are going with Marie to Vienna. But Anne Seymour, Louise Redfield, Viole Allison, Elsie Carr, Dorothy Brentham, and Ruth Wynyard. You will be the only prefect there, Joey. Oh, and, of course, Eustacia Benson.'

'I knew it,' groaned Jo. 'It's no use trying to be casual about it, Madge. It's simply awful.'

Madge freed one hand from the Robin's grasp, and slipped it under the pointed chin, to turn up to hers the clever face she loved so dearly. 'Jo, don't you think you are being very unkind and unselfish? I know Eustacia is not the kind of girl you like, but, remember, she is newly an orphan; she has only this aunt to love her; she has been brought up to be unlovable, and she has been pitchforked into a quite new atmosphere. *Any* girl would have found this difficult at first. But for a girl of her peculiar temperament it must have been more than difficult. Now, I want you to try to put aside your own feelings and do your best to persuade her to be friends with you this exeat. You can do it if you try. Will you?'

'It's hard lines on me,' grumbled Jo.

'I know that. Still, will you do it?'

'I'll think about it,' was all she got. But Madge was satisfied. Jo would do her best to help Eustacia now, she knew. Then she turned to the small person on her lap. 'And what will Robin do? You can't go climbing, my dearie, but you will find that someone will always stay with you, and you need have no fear of being lonely. When the others go off for the day, will you be happy, and not be too sorry that you are not at the Sonnalpe with papa?'

'Me—I will be good,' sighed the Robin, with an extra tight hug.

'And, anyway, I'll stay with you,' promised Joey. 'We don't see each other much in term-time, do we, *mein Blümchen*?'

'Not every day, Joey,' said Madge. 'I want you to see the glacier. But you may stay with her on the Friday and the Monday. Sunday, of course, you will all be at the *Gasthaus*'.

'All right,' agreed Jo. 'Someone else will stay with her on Saturday, I suppose. And what about Tuesday?'

'You will come down into Innsbruck on Tuesday,' said her sister. 'Some of the girls don't know it very well, so you will spend the day there. You two are going to the Maranis for *Mittagessen*, and the Menches for *Kaffee*. Then Frieda and Maria will join you, and you will all come back together. But it is all three weeks away, and I don't want you to worry about it yet. Here comes Luise with *Kaffee und Kuchen*, and we are going to have a cosy little party to ourselves.

It was not until the meal was nearly over that Joey remarked casually, 'By the way, what do you think of the feud?'

'Feud? What feud?' asked Madge quickly.

'Between the Fourth and Fifth. Of course, they are little asses, still it's rather—upsetting.'

'How did it happen?'

'Something to do with Eustacia's pen. I haven't heard all the details. But Margia and Evvey are mixed up in it, and the forms are at daggers drawn. It was Ch—er—Miss Stewart's fault.'

'Nonsense!' said Madge crisply. 'If it was anyone's fault, it was one of the forms!'

'I suppose you'd have to say that,' sighed Jo. 'Well, who-ever is to blame, there's trouble all round, and they are hating each other good and hard. They can't even be civil to each other!'

Madge frowned. 'I wish you girls would try to make allowances for each other occasionally! I never heard of anything so absurd! We never seem to get quiet terms here at all!' Just then a tap at the door told them that some-one wanted Mrs. Russell.

'Go and see who it is, Jo,' said her sister.

Jo went, and disclosed Miss Wilson, who had come for a chat.

'Come in, Miss Wilson,' cried Madge, turning her head. —'Run away now, my pets.'

The pair said good-bye reluctantly and went off, leaving the two ladies together.

All thing considered, the short visit was entirely a suc-cess, and Madge went back happy in the knowledge that she had left Jo and the Robin fairly contented with their half-term lot. It is true the Robin shed a few tears when she said 'Good-bye', but she was not given to fretting over what could not be helped, and was soon her sunny little self again.

Even Eustacia seemed to be happier than she had been, and Madge left, congratulating herself on the fact that things seemed likely to go well till the end of term. She never made a bigger mistake. The very worst things of all were yet to come.

Chapter XV

HALF-TERM BEGINS

'LAST lesson for five days! Hurrah!' And Evadne tossed up her French grammar and caught it again, scattering loose leaves round her as she did so.

"What an age Mademoiselle Lachenais is!" exclaimed Ilonka.

'P'r'aps she isn't coming,' suggested Elsie. Then, as the sound of footsteps in the corridor outside came to them, 'Oh, yes; here she is!'

Mademoiselle Lachenais, a vivacious little French-woman, entered the room just as Evadne had picked up the last page and was wishing her form *'Bon jour, mes enfants!'* in her crisp accents. The form settled down to translation lesson with some impatience, for they were far too excited about the long half-term exeat to bother with French, and Mademoiselle had need of all her patience and tact that afternoon. Somehow the lesson dragged to its close, and then, when the bell rang at half-past fifteen, there was a general sigh of relief. *Kaffee* was to be at sixteen, and then they would set off with torches and lanterns for Spärtz, at the foot of the mountain.

Small wonder, then, that the girls chattered eagerly as they took their *Kaffee* and cakes, and that even the Robin, who had come over with those left of the juniors for the meal, was nearly wild with excitement. It seemed to the girls as though the staff would *never* finish eating; but at length Mademoiselle rang the bell for Luise, and they were dismissed to change into hats and coats, and scarves and gloves, and then had to range themselves for inspection, so that she might see that they were all clad with sufficient warmth. That over, she bade them all good-bye and wished them a happy time, and they set off. It was not quite dark in the valley, but once they had reached the path that winds down the mountain-side to Spärtz, and came under the pines that fringe it, they were glad of their torches and lanterns to show them the way. They sang marching songs as they went, and the elders helped the little ones. All the same, Miss Wilson whispered to her friend that she was glad their party were to spend the night at the great Europe hotel in Innsbruck, going up to Fulpmes on the Stubaital-bahn the next day.

In the train the Robin promptly fell asleep, and some of the others were not slow in following her example; Miss Stewart negatived Joey's suggestion of waking the baby as they neared the outskirts of Innsbruck, and the small girl found herself in a bedroom in the hotel when she did rouse up.

Joey and Elsie and Anne spent a thoroughly satisfactory evening with the Maranis, and returned to the hotel very sleepy, but very happy. Eustucia, Louise, and Violet had gone to the Rincinis, and the last two had been invited to the Mensches. Herr Mensch brought them back to the Europe, and then stole upstairs to look at the Robin, who lay, rosy and dimpled, in a sound sleep. She and Joey would always be dear to them, for they had known and loved *die Grossmutter*, who had loved them in return. He kissed the small girl tenderly, and then told Joey that in the holidays he and Frau Mensch hoped to have the pair with them. 'But not this time,' he rumbled softly, with an eye on the sleeping Robin. 'It is too near the last time when *die Mutter* kissed and blessed our little angel.'

Joey nodded, with a lump in her throat. 'She's got her own baby now,' she whispered.

The kindly giant smiled. 'Yes; she never forgot my little sister. As you say, *mein Kind*, she has her own now. But it is late, and you ought to sleep. *Gute Nacht, mein Blümchen.*'

'*Gute Nacht*,' repeated Jo, holding up her face for his kiss. Then he went, and she tumbled into bed as quickly as she could.

The next morning, to quote Jo, the real excitement began, when, after they had had *Frühstück*, they tucked their night-things into their cases, and set off through the snowy streets for the Stubaitalbahn. Along the Maria-Theresien Strasse they went, turning into the Maximilian-Strasse. Then they turned again, along the Andreas Hofer Strasse, and so up to the Westbahnhof, an electric tram taking them through Wilten, the pretty little suburb of Innsbruck. There they alighted, and walked briskly through the streets till they came to the Stubaital-Bahnhof, where they would take the electric-cable train to Fulpmes, at the foot of the great Stubai It was a long walk, but, for the sake of the new girls, Miss Stewart thought it well worth doing, so that they might see as much of Innsbruck as possible. If they tired too soon, it was always possible to get a tram; and their cases had been sent on to Fulpmes that morning, so they had nothing to carry but small handbags.

In the Andreas Hofer Strasse, Joey retailed the story of the great Tyrolean patriot with much vivid detail, for she was devoted to his memory, even though it told against her own hero, Napoleon. The others listened enraptured, and begged for more.

Eustacia, however, was moved to improve the occasion. 'I have never been able to understand why so many people must think Napoleon great,' she observed. 'I consider he was just a brutal domineering tyrant.'

Joey flared up at once. 'He was one of the greatest men the world has ever seen!' she cried. 'He had no idea what his men were doing to poor old Hofer till it was too late. And he made the French a nation, and a *great* nation!'

Eustacia stared at her. 'I do not think you are very patriotic to speak so of one who was one of the greatest of England's enemies,' she said.

'One can always admire a man, whether he is on one's side or not,' retorted Jo. 'Napoleon was a very great man. He was a fine general, and a great leader. He *made* modern France after the French Revolution had left it in pieces. And what do *you* know about him, anyway? You always say that you know next to no history, and that learning it is a waste of time.'

Eustacia smiled in a superior way. 'So it is—as we are taught it. And I cannot say I think much of your choice in heroes, since you can admire a man who was merely a good soldier.'

'And what else were Achilles and Hector, and all the other Greek and Trojan idiots you pretend to think so much of?' demanded Jo.

Before Eustacia could reply, however, Miss Wilson came up to them, to ask Joey if she did not want to go to Fulpmes, since she was marching past the Bahnhof.

That awoke the pair of them to the fact that they had reached the Stubaitalbahn, and they followed the mistress into the ticket office, outwardly very meek, but inwardly boiling.

The railway runs round and round the mountain-side, frequently crossing valleys on high bridges, running slowly, and stopping now and then at the little villages through which the road has been built.

They were soon out of sight of the Sill valley as the railway wound on round the mountain through Natters and Mutters, and then into the short dark tunnel which comes before Nockhofweg. They crossed the Mühlbach, and so on and on, till presently they were passing through a wood where the bare branches of the trees were still laden with snow, and what were in summer pleasant meadows were now plains of whiteness, till at length the little engine drew up before the platform of the Bahnhof of Fulpmes. Here they all tumbled out, and Miss Wilson looked round for someone to direct them to their pension. There are several good hotels in Fulpmes, but most of them close after September ends, since the season is then over, and they had had to arrange for a pension.

A tall lanky fellow, in faded green coat and breeches, with huge shawl-like scarf wound round his shoulders, came forward, hat in hand, to bow, and ask in a pleasant voice if these were the gracious ladies for the Pension Gisela.

Miss Wilson thanked him, and asked him to lead the way. He went ahead, and presently they found themselves outside a tall, square house, with green jalousies set back from the windows, and a bright yellow door, which, at their arrival, was flung open by a huge woman with a good-natured face and a welcoming smile. She greeted them cheerfully, drew them all in, exclaiming at their temerity in making a visit to the Stubai-Tal in such weather, and led them into a long narrow room, where a huge porcelain stove gave out a heat that was grateful to the people who had been freezing steadily in the train on the slow journey up.

'*Mittagessen* will be ready very soon,' said their hostess, who had introduced herself as Frau Blitzen. 'The baggage has already arrived, and it is set in the rooms I have put all ready for you. Will you come, gracious ladies, and see how they will suit you?'

They followed up the steep narrow staircase, along an equally narrow passage, and so to four rooms, whose doors she flung open, exclaiming, 'Here—and here! And here for the young ladies. I have put this cot for the little one'.

Everything was very bare, the furniture being reduced to the minimum, but everything was exquisitely clean; the linen of driven-snow whiteness; the floor waxed and polished to the last degree; the window sparkling with frost ferns. Stoves in the corner of each room were lit, and made the rooms warm and comfortable. On the whitewashed walls hung one or two pictures—for the most part copies of the Holy Family. The neat beds had plumeaux on them in red covers, which gave a cosy aspect to the room.

Jo beamed as she looked round. 'Topping, isn't it, Anne?'

'Splendid,' said Anne. 'I never saw a room like this before. Only, how *are* we going to wash?'

'Oh, we'll manage,' said Jo easily. 'They never do give you more than a pudding-basin to wash in.'

'I hear the bell, Joey,' put in the Robin. 'Can we go? I am so hungry!'

'Rather! So'm I,' said Joey. 'Come on, you two!'

They left the room, to be met in the passage by the others, and ran downstairs to the *Gastzimmer*, where bowls of soup awaited them.

The soup was followed by pink boiled ham served with prunes. This course ended, there came plates of something that looked, and tasted, not unlike porridge, and with this they ate cherries steeped in spirits. The whole was topped off by excellent coffee and rolls split and spread with jam of some kind. Eustacia looked rather askance at this queer mixture, and Miss Wilson saw to it that the Robin had only two cherries; but the others enjoyed it all with keen appetite.

When the meal was ended, they were sent off to unpack their cases, and then they all put on their wraps and set off to find one of the many guides who live in the village, to arrange with him for an expedition on the morrow.

Johannes Siebur stared when he found that he was expected to take two ladies and a party of school-girls under his wing. He protested that this was not the weather for *die Damen* to go climbing. But Miss Wilson, helped out by Joe, whose patois was as fluent as her classic German, managed to persuade him, and he agreed to take them up the Frohneben Alp on the morrow. This was an easy walk, he said, and would not tire them too much. He also agreed to take them to some point on the Stubai glacier on the Monday if the weather were fitting; and for the Tuesday, suggested that they should go to Mieders, as they would have to leave Fulpmes in the early afternoon, in order to catch the train to Spärtz.

'That will do very nicely, indeed. We mustn't miss that train,' said Miss Wilson, little guessing what Tuesday was to bring forth. 'Then we will be here by half-past nine tomorrow morning, and you will be ready for us?'

'*Ja, gnädiges Fräulein*,' replied the guide. 'And—the *gnädiges Fräulein* will pardon—how many will go?'

'Nine of us,' replied Miss Wilson. 'All, save the baby and one other who will stay to watch her.'

' '*Sist gut*,' he replied; and then wished them '*guten Tag*', and retired into his house.

'I'll stay with the Robin tomorrow, Miss Wilson,' said Jo. 'I promised her. My sister said I should go out on Monday and Tuesday, though. Will someone else take those days?'

'I'll take Monday, if you like,' proposed Anne promptly.

'That will do very nicely,' said Miss Wilson. 'And Tuesday will probably arrange itself.'

'It's going to be a fine night, I think,' said Miss Stewart, as they turned to walk back to their pension. 'Those mountains must look magnificent under moonlight. They make even our great crags at Tiernsee look small, don't they?'

'If it's fine, we'll walk down the valley before supper,' promised Miss Wilson. 'But come along now, you people. It's growing dusk, and I'm hungry again.—Tired, Robin? Like a ride on my back?'

'I can walk quite well, thank you,' said the Robin, with a broad beam. 'Oh, I *do* like this dear little place! There's the church! Do we all go there on Sunday?'

'I suppose so,' replied Miss Wilson, as she took the small hand slipped into hers. 'Anne and Louise and Dorothy and you, at any rate. Joey may if she likes. I know her sister doesn't mind.'

'Rather not,' said Joey, who was striding along on the other side of the Robin. 'She has more sense than to be narrow-minded about *that*! What about Elsie and Vi and Ruth and Eustacia, though?'

'Elsie may go if she chooses. Her mother has sent written permission,' replied the mistress. 'I don't think we'll take Violet or Ruth. I don't know about Eustacia.'

'I'll ask her!' And Jo called back a melodious 'Eustacia!'

'You want me?' inquired the young lady.

'Yes; will you come to Mass with us on Sunday? Or will you stay at home with Vi and Ruth?'

Eustacia stopped dead in the middle of the path, causing Anne, who was not expecting it and who was rather near her, nearly to fall over her.

'Of course I shall not go!' she said indignantly.

'Oh, all right. Keep your hair on,' said Joey easily. 'I only *asked* you, you know.' She turned back to Miss Wilson

96

with a cheerful remark about the next day's plans, and had forgotten both question and answer within five minutes.

But Eustacia had not, and was still indignant when they went up the steps of the pension and scattered to their rooms to make themselves tidy once more before going down for *Kaffee und Kuchen*. She was quickly ready, and then made her way along the passage to the room shared by Jo, Anne, and the Robin. And and the Robin were ready, but Jo was not when she tapped.

'I'll go down with Robin, Joey,' said Anne. 'You and Eustacia can follow.'

The pair departed, and Eustacia closed the door carefully after them, and stood watching Joey gloomily as she changed. 'Why should you wish to take me to the Catholic church?' she demanded abruptly.

Joey stared at her in unqualified amazement. 'Don't be so silly! I only asked if you wished to come with us. I'm going; they usually have glorious singing in these little churches. And, after all, Eustacia, it's only *one* of the roads to God. If you think that way, then it's best for you. If you think another way, then *that's* best. But they all go to the same end.'

'Are you a Catholic?'

Joey shook her head. 'I am not. You know very well that I'm C. of E.'

'I don't believe you,' returned Eustacia.

'Oh, all right! Say I'm telling lies, and have done with it!' Eustacia made no reply to this.

'Silly little ass!' went on Jo, who was ruffled by the other girl's calm superiority.

Eustacia flushed up. Of all the girls at the Chalet School, Joey Bettany was the one who had most power to annoy her. She never stopped to inquire why this was so, and if anyone had told her that it was because Jo was the one she most cared for, she would have been incredulous. 'I will not be called names!' she flamed out.

'Then don't go hinting that I'm a liar. Come on! *Kaffee* will be in, and we shall be fearfully late.'

Eustacia followed her, not quite knowing what else to do; but she was still angry at the contemptuous epithet Jo had flung at her, and made up her mind to get her own back somehow. Joey Bettany should know before long that she was not a person to be treated with contempt, and on that point she was decided. The only thing was, she couldn't quite make up her mind how she was to do it.

After *Kaffee*, Miss Stewart suddenly realised that this queer new child had been very silent, and smilingly teased her about it. There was no malice in her teasing; but Eustacia was so unaccustomed to anything of the sort that she saw real unkindness in it, and grew angrier and angrier. Finally, she refused to go out again when the others did, and, since the Robin had trotted off to bed at her usual early hour long before they had departed, she was left to herself.

'Give an eye to Robin, won't you?' were Joey's parting words as they left.

Eustacia muttered something which might have passed for agreement, and Jo went off, happy about the child. She had forgotten all about the squabble before *Kaffee*, and would have thought nothing about it, even if she had remembered. Hers was not a nature to bear malice. She could be furiously angry; but it was soon over, and then she never even thought of it again. That Eustacia should be brooding over the affair never occurred to her, and she would have laughed to scorn any suggestion to that effect.

Unfortunately Eustacia was the direct opposite. She held on to grudges and was inclined to be vengeful. Thus, while most of the others were walking gaily down the valley chattering about what they meant to do during the week-end, she was sitting in the *Gastzimmer*, a book before her but her mind far away, thinking out a revenge that would hurt Jo Bettany badly, and make her realise that Eustacia Benson was someone to reckon with.

Chapter XVI

SATURDAY AND SUNDAY

It was late when the walking-party got in, and Eustacia had betaken herself to bed, still thinking about her revenge. Hot milky coffee and buttered rolls were waiting for them, and when they had eaten their fill the girls were sent off to bed.

'Bedtime, and more than bedtime!' said Miss Wilson, laughing.

They ran up the stairs laughing and calling, for there were no other guests to be considered, and the Robin was likely to sleep through any noise they might make.

As they came to the door of the room where Eustacia was domiciled, Jo opened it and stuck in an untidy head. 'Hello, Eustacia!' she said. 'You missed a treat, I can tell you. It's a gorgeous night—full of stars! If we have a walk on Sunday and it's like this, you *must* come!'

Louise and Elsie pulled her away from the door, and entered themselves.

'Better get off to bed,' said Louise. 'Bill told us to go, and you know what she is!'

'Bill won't be too squelching this week-end,' laughed Jo. 'Still, it might be as well.—Good-night, Eustacia.—Good-night, you two!'

'Good-night!' chorused the pair; but Eustacia spoke never a word.

Joey removed herself to her own room, and speedily undressed and fell asleep under the crimson-covered plumeau. Anne slumbered peacefully at her side, and the Robin never winked an eyelash.

They were sound asleep when Miss Wilson came across in the morning to call them, and she laughed as she looked at them from the doorway. 'Wake up, sleepy-heads! Do you intend to sleep all day? Miss Stewart and I have been dressed quite a long time.'

Joey sat up with a bang. 'Goodness! What time is it?' she demanded.

'Nearly eight o'clock. Get up, and hurry about it!'

Anne yawned under the bedclothes. 'O-oh! I'm so sleepy!'

'You'll be all right once you get up,' said Miss Wilson unfeelingly.—'Come, my Robin; tumble out!'

The rooms were not cold, but they were not warm. Anne tucked herself into a dressing-gown, and while Joey scrambled into her clothes, proceeded to attend to the Robin's wants.

Jo was quick, and was ready long before the little girl had reached the washing stage. 'I'll take over now, Anne,' she said. 'You buck up—and dress warmly. You'll need it!'

When they were ready they went out into the passage, where they were met by Elsie, in brown skirt and yellow jumper, her pretty, wavy hair plaited back from her face and rolled up over her ears to keep it out of her way during the climb. Anne had done the same thing at Jo's suggestion; Louise, who was shingled, had not had to bother. Eustacia was not ready yet; and Elsie giggled as she told the others of that young lady's remarks on the inadequacy of the washing arrangements.

'She got all hot and bothered,' chuckled Elsie, leading the way downstairs. 'You *should* have heard her on the subject!'

Miss Wilson and Miss Stewart came in a moment later, clad for the expedition in climbing knickers and jumpers.

'All here?' asked Miss Stewart.

'All but Eustacia,' said Jo. 'Shall I run up and hurry her up?'

'Yes, run along, Joey,' said Miss Wilson.

Joey went off, calling as she went, 'Eustacia—Eusta-cia! Buck up! You're late!'

Eustacia met her at the door of the room. She wore the brown skirt and yellow knitted jumper which were part of the school uniform; but she had done her hair into its usual two tight plaits, and they hung primly down her back.

'I say, you'd better roll your hair up,' said Joey in her friendly way. 'It'll be an awful nuisance like that when you are climbing.'

'Will you kindly keep your personal remarks to yourself, Jo Bettany?' snapped Eustacia.

Joey stared. 'You ass! I wasn't being personal; I was only giving you advice!'

'And don't call me names, either! I won't submit to it!'

'Keep your hair on!' said Jo lightly. 'didn't say anything very awful. If "silly ass" is the worst you're ever called in your life, you won't come off so badly!'

Eustacia drew herself up, her thin lips pressed together in a straight line; her eyes gleaming. 'I will not be insulted by you or anyone else. If you go on with this sort of behaviour, I shall report the matter to Miss Wilson, and so I warn you!'

'Oh, rats!' retorted Jo. 'You do lose your balance so! *Frühstück* is ready, so come along! You don't want cold coffee, do you?'

Eustacia did not; she also saw that Jo was not affected in the least by her words; so she went down, feeling thoroughly furious. She was very silent all the time they were eating, and took no part in the merry chatter that went on during the meal.

When it was over, Miss Wilson gave Joey instructions for the day, and then went off to get into her cap and long-skirted coat and nailed shoes. 'Take care of Robin, Joey,' she said, when she came down again and found the whole of the party waiting for her in the hall. 'Don't go too far anywhere, and be sure you are back at the proper time for *Mittagessen.*—And Robin, you must be obedient to Joey, and be sure you get your afternoon nap, *mein Vögelein.*'

'Me, I will be good,' the Robin assured her. 'And I will do all that you say.'

'I know,' said 'Bill', bending down to kiss the rosy face. 'Now we must go.—Good-bye, you two, and don't get into any mischief while we are away.—I don't know how long we shall be, Joey, but we shall be back by nineteen at the latest. Robin must go to bed at her usual time, of course.'

Joey nodded, and, after directing Eustacia to tuck her plaits out of the way, the mistress gave the word to set out, and they went off to seek their guide. Joey and the Robin waved to them from the open door and, when they were out of sight, withdrew to the *Gastzimmer.*

And what will you do today, *meine Kinder*?' inquired good Frau Blitzen, pausing in her task of clearing the table.

'I think we'll go and see the village properly this morning,' said Joey. 'Then, this afternoon, I'll read while Robin is sleeping, and when she gets up we'll go up the valley a little. What time is *Mittagessen*, please?'

'At twelve,' replied their hostess.

'We'll go and put on our things and have a look at the village. Is there anything special to see, *meine Frau*?'

'But yes; there are the iron and steel works,' said Frau Blitzen. 'My Fritz is *Obermeister* at the Florian works. Go there, and tell him that I have sent you, and then he will ask permission that you see everything. And there is the little shop kept by Hans Lange. He carves wonderful wooden toys that the baby would like to see.'

The Robin beamed at the idea, and Joey thanked the good lady prettily before she led her small charge upstairs to put on her outdoor clothes. Presently they were both walking briskly over the frozen snow, rejoicing in the pale February sunlight that made the ice-crystals sparkle like a thousand diamonds.

'Where do we go first, dearest?' asked the small maid.

'I vote we go and find that old man first,' said Joey. 'I thought he sounded jolly interesting. We might get some things to take home for Madge and Jem and Uncle Ted. He might have something we could take David, too.'

'And there will be Onkel Dick and Tante Mollie, and the twins and Biddy,' supplemented the Robin, who had calmly adopted Madge Russell's twin brother and his wife and babies on their first coming to the Tyrol.

'So there are!' exclaimed Jo. 'Well, we'll have a stiff time making our money hang out!'

Hans Lange's prices were very low and they were able to get a gift of some kind for everyone.

After they had bidden him '*Grüss Gott*' in the pretty Tyrolean style, they left him beaming still, and took the road for the great ironworks where Herr Blitzen worked. They spent so long that they were late for *Mittagessen*, even though they ran most of the way back. When the meal was over, Joey took the Robin upstairs and tucked her into her cot for the afternoon nap that was rarely missed. Her mother had died of tuberculosis, brought on by the privations during the war in Poland, and the child was very frail. Dr Jem had made a special study of her, and put her on a strict régime. She was improving tremendously under it, and they hoped that, if it were maintained during the whole of her early years, she would escape the horrid thing. Plenty of sleep, plenty of fresh air, and any amount of milk formed the main parts of it; and this midday sleep was a most important item. After resting, they went down for *Kaffee*, which was waiting for them.

'We're going up the valley now, Frau Blitzen,' Joey said, as that worthy dame came in to see that they had everything they wanted. 'May we have milk when we returrn? It will be about eighteen then. I'll wait supper for the others, if they haven't come back; but Robin must go to bed.'

It was nearly nineteen when the climbers returned, bringing with them accounts of a glorious walk over the snow and a climb that had not been too easy.

On Sunday Mass was celebrated at ten, and those girls who were to attend had to get ready as soon as *Frühstück* was over. Eustacia stayed with Violet and Ruth, and Miss Stewart stayed with them.

When the church party had returned they waited for the other four to get ready, and then went for a brisk walk up the valley, which occupied the time till *Mittagessen* very nicely.

'What do you want to do this afternoon?' asked Miss Wilson, as they were returning.

'Oh, walk, of course!' said Joey instantly. 'Can't we have *Kaffee* later, and be out all the time the daylight lasts?'

'Yes, if you like,' replied Miss Wilson. 'How would it be to go by train to Natters, and look round? We could get *Kaffee* somewhere there, surely.—Joey, run and ask Frau Blitzen if she would come and advise us.'

Joey ran off, and presently returned with Frau Blitzen, who smoothed out their difficulties with delightful ease. Certainly they could go to Natters. As for the *Kaffee*, did not her sister live there, and would she not be delighted to give *Kaffee und Kuchen* to the English ladies? She herself —Frau Blitzen—would write a note for them to take down, and then Moidl, her sister, better known as Frau Alphen, would do all in her power to help them.

'Frau Alphen?' queried Joey, her quick ears catching the name. 'Any relation to Herr Alphen, the hairdresser in Innsbruck?'

'But yes, *mein Kind*. He is her husband,' replied Frau Blitzen.

'Oh then, I know him,' said Joey instantly. 'I'm sure he'll

remember us if I remind him of how Grizel asked him for *holy* water to rinse her hair.'

'*Bitte?*' said Frau Blitzen in bewilderment, wondering if she had heard aright.

'Years ago,' said Jo solemnly, 'when we first came here, we had with us a friend who got mixed up with "*Heisses*" *Wasser* and "*Heiliges*" *Wasser*. Herr Alphen's face was a treat! Madge and I simply collapsed!'

'Poor Grizel!' said Miss Wilson, laughing. 'I hope you didn't tease her too much about it!'

'Madge wouldn't let me,' said Joey ruefully. 'She said that anyone coming fresh to the country and the language might have made the same mistake. But it was priceless to see him.'

'I see nothing funny about it.' This was Eustacia's contribution to the conversation. 'The two words are remarkably similar, and I consider it rather ill-bred to laugh at an innocent error.'

'D'you mean Madge?' demanded Jo, swinging round on her at once.

Luckily, Miss Wilson intervened at that moment. 'Girls! Go to your rooms, and make yourselves tidy at once. *Mittagessen* will be ready shortly, and you all look disgraceful.'

They went off, but Jo was still fuming at the bare idea that anyone could call her beloved sister 'ill-bred'. There could be no doubt about it, Eustacia and Joey were rubbing one another up the wrong way most strenuously, and it would be strange if there were not bad trouble between them before the exeat was over.

Chapter XVII

THE STUBAI GLACIER

THE rest of Sunday passed fairly quietly. Jo and Eustacia could scarcely speak to one another without coming to a clash; still, that was nothing to worry about. Eustacia must shake down into her proper place, and it would do Jo no harm to realise that other people might have different views from herself. So far, she had had things a good deal her own way, and had been a leader among the girls. Eustacia certainly had no intention of falling under her charm, whatever her subconscious feelings might be. Of all the Chaletians, Jo Bettany was the one who was most easily able to ruffle her, and she came to the conclusion that, much as she disliked most of the others, it was Jo who bore off the palm. By the time 'Bill' ordered them off to bed, the new girl was seething with rage, and only longing for something that would enable her to show her dislike.

Next morning they were called at the unearthly hour of half-past four. Herr Siebur had arranged to meet them at half-past five if the weather were fine, and he had come at twenty the previous night to say that there was every indication of a fine day coming, and they must be ready for him.

Eustacia loved her bed, and she detested this early rising. She grumbled while she was dressing, and when 'Bill' sent her upstairs again to tuck up her long plaits, she grumbled more.

Herr Siebur was waiting for them, and he at once ranged alongside of Miss Wilson and informed her that the day was likely to be very fine indeed, and he thought it might be quite possible to get to the glacier—at any rate, near enough for the girls to see it.

'Oh, topping!' cried Joey joyfully.

'Isn't it thrilling?' chuckled Elsie. 'I've never been close to a glacier in all my life! This will be something to write home about, won't it?'

That was the general feeling, and the girls went on gaily, though some of the more inexperienced people were inclined to grumble at the slow pace set by the guide.

'We'll never get there at this rate,' proclaimed Ruth.

Joey, who was walking in front with Louise, turned round. 'Oh yes, we will,' she said. 'If we dashed ahead as you want to do, we'd be done at the end of an hour, and *then* we should never get there! Have to sit down to rest every few minutes. You don't know what you're talking about, my child!'

Ruth sniffed and tossed her head, but she said no more. Eustacia, on the other hand, who happened to be walking beside her, rushed into the fray, irritated by Jo's cocksure manner. 'You always appear to think you know better than anyone else,' she remarked.

Jo laughed. 'In this instance, I *do*. I've been here for some time now, and I've done quite a lot of climbing. Ruth has done next to none. That's all there is to it.'

Eustacia sniffed and went on in silence, while Ruth, after relieving her feelings by pulling a face at Jo, resumed the slow, steady walk of which she had complained, and they went forward.

By this time the sky was paling towards the east, and stars were twinkling less brightly. A chill wind blew down on them from the glacier, bringing with it the indescribable sour smell of wet ice.

'Dawn coming,' said Miss Wilson. 'Presently we shall pause for a while and have some of our coffee and rolls. Then we shall go on till we reach the hut, and we will rest there for half an hour. After that, no more stops till we reach the glacier. I'm afraid we can't cross it, but you will *see* it, and that's what matters today.'

Gradually, the grey in the east became tinged with a rosy light. The dusk fled away, and they walked on in the warmth of the rising sun.

'Look at the snow-caps of the mountains!' said Louise suddenly. 'They're pink—*pink—pink!*'

'Glorious!' murmured Jo, gazing round at the beauty, with all her heart in her eyes.

'It is really wonderful,' came Eustacia's stilted accents behind them, effectually crushing all rapture.

It was still sunrise when they sat down and at their buttered rolls and drank the hot coffee which was in their Thermos flasks. Herr Siebur sat at a little distance from them, munching at a sandwich, composed of a roll with a chunk of Württemberger sausage inserted. Jo sat in a heap on a snowy rock, with Louise beside her, and Eustacia and Ruth at her feet. 'Here's to our climb!' she cried suddenly, waving her collapsible cup in the air. 'May——'

What next she would have said will never be known, for at that moment the cup collapsed, and Eustacia was deluged with the hot coffee. She yelled, and so did Jo, who was startled by the sudden shower-bath she had inflicted on the new girl.

Miss Wilson leapt to her feet and hurried forward to investigate matters. 'Joey! What on earth were you doing? What possessed you to wave your cup about like that?— Are you hurt, Eustacia?'

'I'm—I'm all wet!' stammered Eustacia. 'All that hot coffee. I wish I'd never come!—You did it on purpose, Josephine Bettany!'

Joey stared. 'I say, that's rot,' she said seriously. 'I never meant to wet you. It was an accident. I never thought the beastly thing would go in like that. I say, I hope you aren't scalded or anything like that? Let me mop you up.'

'It *wasn't* an accident!' raged Eustacia. 'You did it on purpose! You are always doing things like that to me! But you needn't think you can always do it, because I shall jolly well pay you back——'

'Eustacia! Be quiet!' cried Miss Wilson, breaking in on the torrent of words. 'Have you taken leave of your senses? Come here, and let me dry you, child. And kindly don't talk like that again. Of course it was an accident.—Though I must say, Joey, it was one that might have been avoided. What possessed you to swing the thing like that?'

But Eustacia was in a flaming temper, and she didn't care who knew it. 'Of course you take Jo Bettany's side!' she exclaimed. 'You all do—always. It's rank favour-itism——'

'Be quiet at once,' said Miss Wilson sternly. 'How dare you speak to a mistress like that?—Joey, kindly finish your coffee—the rest of you as well.—Eustacia, stand still!'

Her voice calmed the excited Eustacia a little. Miss Wilson had rarely spoken in such a tone to any girl all the time she had been at the Chalet School.

'Bill' dried Eustacia as well as she could, with a grim face and compressed lips. She said no more, but there was a chill in the air that had nothing to do with the climate. When the girl was ready, she marshalled her little band into order once more, and gave them the word to march on. They went in silence for a while; then the rapidly brightening light and the mountain air, like champagne, restored their spirits, and their tongues began to wag once more, at first shyly, then with the usual freedom. Only Eustacia said nothing. She stalked along in bitter silence at Ruth's side, and that happy-go-lucky young lady wished heartily that she had another partner.

It was well on in the morning before they came to the hut built for the convenience of Alpinists at the foot of the glacier, and looked down on the frozen glacier stream, which in summer was a grey river of running water; now it was stilled by the mighty frost king. Great boulders lay about, marking the terminal moraine, and they knew that more lay on either side of the glacier itself.

Normally a rough path led up by the lateral moraines, but now it was buried beneath the whiteness of the snow, and they had a long, tough struggle before they were above the glacier and looking across. Now the queer, sour smell was more noticeable than ever. The sun's rays, striking across the ice, turned it to a thousand diamonds. But it was not white, as many of them had supposed it would be, it was a greenish-blue, even more wonderful to see.

For ten minutes Herr Siebur let them look, then he came up to Miss Wilson and said something in a low tone, pointing, as he spoke, over his right shoulder. The mistress turned and looked. In the sky, hitherto clear, were some yellowish clouds, coming up with slow determination. She uttered an exclamation. She knew what those clouds might mean. 'Girls,' she said, 'we must get back now! Fall into rank, and turn back.—Miss Stewart, will you lead, please? I will tail off.'

Joey looked at the mistress's face, but 'Bill' had her features well under control, and there was nothing to be learnt there. The prefect turned to look at the sky, and her own face became grave. She knew the danger now. Those clouds meant snow—and heavy snow at that. They must not be caught out on the mountain-side. Without a word she went back to Violet Allison, who was showing signs of strain, and tucked the younger girl's arm through hers. 'Come on, Vi. I'll give you a hand down here,' she said cheerfully.—'Louise,' raising her voice, 'you might do the same by Elsie.'

Louise nodded, and came to Elsie at once. Miss Stewart had taken Ruth in charge, and Dorothy was on the other side of her. 'Bill' had insisted on Eustacia's taking her arm, and, thus arranged, they made all possible speed down the mountain.

'What is it, Joey?' asked Violet presently.

'I don't quite know,' said Joey, 'but it looks as though a blizzard might be coming up.'

Violet, an imaginative, nervy child, shuddered. 'Oh, Joey, how awful!'

At this point Herr Siebur came back to Jo, and, without a word, picked up the younger girl, lifting her across

108

his shoulder in such a way as to make the burden of her light weight as easy as possible. Then he strode on again. The clouds were coming up more rapidly now, and they must reach the hut if possible. Once the whirling snow should descend even he, good guide as he was, might find it difficult to locate the place—and these were children, who would not stand exposure.

Seeing that Violet was safe, Joey glanced back to where Eustacia, now very tired, was dragging on 'Bill's' arm. She turned back. 'Take my arm, Eustacia. We'll get on faster that way, I think.'

Eustacia drew back so sharply that she jerked Miss Wilson, who had trodden on a hidden loose stone at that moment. With a sharp cry 'Bill' slipped, tried to steady herself, and went down, twisting her foot under her. She was up again at once, but the involuntary groan she uttered, and her exceeding whiteness, told of some damage.

'Miss Wilson!' cried Jo, catching her as she swayed. 'Are you hurt?'

'Bill' managed to conjure up a smile. 'I've turned my foot a little, Joey. Never mind! Let me lean on you for a few steps. I shall be all right presently.'

'Eustacia, go to the other side!' said Jo sharply.

'I shan't!' flamed Eustacia. 'I'm not going to be ordered about by *you*, Josephine Bettany!'

Joey glared at her. 'You little ass!' she exclaimed. 'Don't you realise that there's a blizzard coming up, and that we must get to the hut if we don't want to die? Take Miss Wilson's other arm, and don't be silly!'

Something in the urgency of her tones frightened Eustacia, and she said no more, but went round to the other side, and between them they contrived to help Miss Wilson on the way.

But the pain of the injured foot was great, and, struggle as she would, 'Bill' felt herself turning faint with it. 'I can't go on!' she gasped. 'Help me to sit down here, and then go on, girls, and ask Herr Siebur to come and help me. He is stronger, and can get me down better.'

Obedience was the first thing in a case of this kind. They settled her on the snow, and Eustacia went off at top speed down the snowy slope. At the same moment a shout told them that the vanguard had reached the hut in safety. Joey came back, and pulling out her handkerchief, stooped down, and began to loosen the heavy boot.

'Joey! What are you doing?' cried Miss Wilson. 'Go at once—the snow will be here in a few minutes!'

'They've reached the hut,' said Joey quietly, drawing off the boot as she spoke.

Miss Wilson made no answer to this. The exquisite pain of the movement finished her, and she collapsed on the side of the road. Joey uttered an exclamation, and then, scraping up some snow, put it on the foot and bound her handkerchief tightly round it. At the same moment she heard a shout, and then Herr Siebur came running up the slope. Not a word did he say, but he stooped and picked up the unconscious Miss Wilson as if she had weighed no more than Violet, and set off down the mountain again, throwing a brief 'Follow!' over his shoulder to Joey, who picked up the boot and tore after him. Already light flakes of snow were falling, and it would take them all their time to reach the hut. They did it—but only just! As they entered, the snow suddenly came in a mad mist of dancing white, and everything outside was veiled from their sight.

Chapter XVIII

A LONG NIGHT

THE first thing to do was to attend to Miss Wilson, and, while Herr Siebur hunted in one of the lockers in the hut for fuel with which to light a fire in the stove, the girls gathered round the mistress. Miss Stewart drew off her stocking and examined the foot. 'A sprain,' she said at length. 'Get some more snow, some of you. We must use it as a compress. I want all the handkerchiefs you can spare, girls, as well.—Give me that scarf, Eustacia, for a pillow.'

Miss Wilson lay back. She was suffering a good deal of pain with her foot, and at present was feeling too poorly to trouble about anything. Herr Siebur left the stove again, having seen that the fire was all right, and hunted through the other lockers to see what food there might be. He found coffee, tins of meat, and some onions and garlic.

A huge pan was found, and Herr Siebur unearthed some tins of condensed milk for coffee. He attended to the cooking, producing a large tin, in which he put the contents of one of the meat-tins, together with some of the onions and a handful of snow. Then, while the girls removed their coats, which were proving rather too warm, now that the stove was going full blast, and made up a bed of them for Miss Wilson, he prepared the coffee; and in less than an hour after they had reached the hut, they were sitting down to very oniony stew, hot coffee, and the remains of their rolls.

'Coo! I didn't know I was so hungry!' said Jo, as she drained the last of her coffee. 'I say! I wonder how long we'll have to stay here.'

'Not very long, I hope,' said Miss Stewart, with an eye on the frailer members of the party. 'However, we certainly can't move yet, so I propose we all lie down and try to get some sleep. Miss Wilson is drowsing just now, but I think she is more comfortable. Joey, you and Louise curl up over here, and Eustacia and Violet next to you.—Ruth and Dorothy, you cuddle down on these coats.—I'll keep watch for a while. In any case, Miss Wilson's foot must be attended to regularly for the present. I'll rouse someone later on when I want to sleep.'

They were all sleepy with the long day in the open air, the warmth of the room, and the hot food they had swallowed. In a very short time Miss Stewart knew herself to be the only wakeful member of the party, and it must be owned that it was only with a struggle that she remained so.

It was midnight by the History mistress's watch when she heard a little stir coming from the corner where the Tyrolean slept, and, looking up, saw him stealing towards her on tiptoe.

'So soon as the night is over I will try to make my way back to Neustift, which is the nearest town, and will bring men and a stretcher, that the gracious lady may be carried down so soon as this storm is ended,' he murmured.

'Will it last long, do you think?' asked Miss Stewart anxiously.

He shook his head. 'It is as the good God wills,' he

replied devoutly. 'I trust not long. The winter is passing quickly, so I think it may be over in two days.'

'*Two days!*' Miss Stewart repeated, aghast. 'But we ought to get to the Tiernsee tomorrow!'

He shook his head. 'We shall be fortunate to leave here on the morrow. And the gracious lady,' he looked down at Miss Wilson again, 'she will not move for many days.'

Miss Stewart's face showed her thoughts, but she said no more. He got up then, and returned to his nook by the stove, and very soon he was snoring again.

Louise roused a little later, and got up carefully, so as not to waken Joey. 'You go and lie down, Miss Stewart,' she said softly. 'I'll stay beside Miss Wilson for a while. You are looking dead, and you ought to rest.'

Miss Stewart, who by this time was completely worn-out, gave way. She crossed the floor on tiptoe, lay down beside Joey, and presently fell into a sound sleep, from which she only wakened when Joey and Eustacia were in the middle of a violent quarrel.

Joey had wakened very stiff and uncomfortable, and when Eustacia, who had roused up in the same condition, began to compain of the discomfort, she flew out at her. 'I *like* your grumbling! It's all your fault that things are like this!'

'*My* fault!' repeated Eustacia in outraged tones. 'Pray, Jo Bettany, did *I* bring on the blizzard?'

'Talk sense!' Joey spoke curtly. 'What I meant was that Bill's accident is your fault. If you hadn't made such a little ass of yourself when I offered to help you, this would never have happened. Now, Bill will most likely have to lie up at Fulpmes for weeks, and it's *your* fault! Don't let me hear you grousing again, or there'll be trouble.'

'I shall do as I like!' retorted Eustacia furiously. 'I'm not going to be bossed by *you*!'

At this point Miss Stewart woke up, and struggled to her feet. 'Girls! Be quiet at once! How dare you squabble like this? You may be very thankful that you are alive and well!'

The morning meal was the same as the night before, but they were hungry again, and ate it thankfully. Miss Stewart kept a wary eye on Violet and Jo. Violet was not strong, and Jo had had a severe attack of pleuro-pneumonia the previous term. Fortunately, beyond looking rather weary, she seemed all right, and Violet looked like her normal self.

What a morning that was! There was nothing to do and nothing to read. They were obliged to be quiet, since 'Bill' was sleeping most of the time, and they had never been so bored in their lives. Finally, Louise suggested that Joey should tell them some of the stories of the Tyrol, and she consented, thankful for something to do.

Herr Siebur had gone an hour before, for the storm had slackened, and he knew the mountain as well as he knew his own kitchen, so there was little fear of him losing his way. The girls gathered to one side of the stove, which he had fed just before he left, and Joey curled up in their midst, and began her stories. 'What sort of stories do you want, anyhow?' she asked.

'*True* stories!' said Ruth, before anyone else could get in a word. 'I don't like all those old fairy-tales of yours; they bore me!'

Jo was breathless at the insult; but Elsie promptly poured oil on troubled waters by saying, 'Tell us some history stories, Jo. Go on! You know dozens of them!'

With a withering glance at matter-of-fact Ruth, Joey stretched herself comfortably, and twisted her mouth in deep thought. 'I'll tell you about the Emperor Maxmilian,' she said finally. She proceeded to tell them a story which occupied and enthralled them for some time.

When she came to the end of it, Eustacia opened her lips to say something especially scathing, but what it was will never be known, for at that moment Violet, who had remained silent all this time, suddenly pointed to the window and cried, 'The sun—the sun! The storm's over at last!'

They all made a dive for the tiny window, and there, sure enough, was the pale light of the sun. While Jo had been telling the story the snow had vanished, and it was bright and fresh outside.

'Can we get off now, Miss Stewart?' asked Louise eagerly. 'Anne and the Robin will be wondering whatever has happened to us.'

Miss Stewart shook her head. 'Not till Herr Siebur returns. We don't know the ways, and the tracks will all be covered again. I don't want any more accidents to happen, thank you, Louise. Miss Wilson is quite enough!' She cast a glance at 'Bill' as she spoke, but 'Bill' was sleeping quietly still.

The girls understood at once, and moved over to the farther side of the hut, where they could talk without fear of rousing her.

'Tell us some more stories, then, Jo,' begged Violet.

'You and stories!' grunted Jo.

'Yes, do! Tell us some legends now,' pleaded Dorothy Brentham. 'The girls all say you know heaps!'

'I dare say! If you want legends, you should ask Frieda Mensch. She has most of them at her finger-ends!'

'But Frieda isn't here,' pointed out Ruth. 'You *are*. Go on, Joey! I think you tell them fine!'

Jo allowed herself to be persuaded, and told them of Andreas Hofer, the great Tyrolean patriot, and of Jakob Stainer, who made the famous Stainer fiddles, and was so enthusiastic about his work that he used to spend whole days in the mountain-forests, listening to the sounds the tree-trunks made as they went down the wood-slides, so that he might choose the best and sweetest for his instruments.

This filled in the time till Miss Stewart called on them to come and help prepare *Mittagessen*. 'We'll have tinned meat without onions this time, I think,' she said, laughing. 'Herr Siebur is a nice man, but he certainly seems to have a passion for onions!'

'And *I* loathe them,' added Joy feelingly.

'You were glad enough to eat them last night—and this morning too,' put in Eustacia, who never seemed to be able to let Jo alone.

'So were you,' said Violet. 'You had two mugfuls last night, 'cos I saw you.'

'I don't talk to children,' said Eustacia loftily.

'I'm no more a child than you are!' retorted Violet heatedly. 'You're only seven months older than I am, Eustacia Benson. So there!'

'Children! Stop this argument!' cried Miss Stewart. 'If there is any more of it, I shall put you all in silence till we get back to the Chalet.'

That calmed them down, and they went about the work in comparative peace. Miss Wilson roused up just as Jo and Louise were pouring the coffee into the mugs, and seemed almost herself again. She was glad that nothing else had happened, and declared that, but for her foot, she herself was quite fit. 'Where is Herr Siebur?' she asked, as she finished her meat.

'He went down to get a stretcher for you from somewhere,' explained Miss Stewart. 'He hoped we might get back to Neustift tonight. From there it will be an easy matter to wire the Chalet, and we must just get back to the Tiernsee as soon as possible.'

'Well—it's no use worrying, I suppose,' said Miss Wilson resignedly.

It obviously wasn't, so after their meal they settled down to an uproarious game of 'General Post', which kept them happy till half-past fourteen brought the sound of voices on the still air, and Louise, who had flown to the window, proclaimed that she could see a party of men coming to them.

'Quick, girls! Tidy up the place and then put on your outdoor things!' said Miss Stewart. 'We can't afford to delay a moment, once they have come. I don't want to be caught on the mountain-slopes after dark.'

They tore about, setting things to rights, and getting into caps and coats and scarves. Eustacia, having forgotten to tuck up her plaits, Jo did it for her, and, for once, the young lady managed to say 'Thank you' quite pleasantly. Louise saw that Violet and Dorothy were properly wrapped up, and Miss Stewart helped Miss Wilson into her coat and cap. There could be no question of putting the boot on the injured foot. The ankle was still terribly swollen, and ached badly.

The men arrived half an hour later and found them all waiting. Joey and Louise had put out the fire in the stove by the simple method of shoving handfuls of snow into it. The smell in the hut was simply awful, but there was no spark left among the wood, as one of the men found when he examined it. A simple stretcher had been brought, and on it a hefty giant of a man laid Miss Wilson, covering her with a blanket that was odorous, to say the least of it. Another made Violet climb on his back, and two more accounted for Dorothy and Ruth. Herr Siebur took up the poles at one end of the stretcher, and the big man who had arranged 'Bill' took up the others. The four remaining were expected to look after themselves to a certain extent, though one man walked with each of them. So arranged they went down the mountain-side through the dying light of the day, and finally reached the head of the valley, where Neustift lies. Here two big sleighs were awaiting them, and they all piled in and were driven swiftly down the valley to Fulpmes, and to good Frau Blitzen, who, with Anne and the Robin, welcomed them with open arms.

The men were well rewarded for their labours, and Herr Siebur went off wondering dazedly whether he had fallen among millionaires. In addition to his normal fees he had been given money equal in value to twenty pounds, and Joey, hearing that he had three little daughters, had demanded his address, so that she might send them each something in return for all their father had done.

Chapter XIX

AFTERWARDS

'ZOE—my Zoë!' And the Robin, falling back on baby pronunciation, leapt into Joey's arms.

'Littlest and best!' murmured Joey, cuddling the baby to her.

'Oh, Zoë, we have missed you so, and when you had not come this morning, I wept! And Anne wept too, and said I might stay up till you came tonight.'

'We were so anxious about you all,' apologised Anne. 'I nearly went off my head last night when you never came. Frau Blitzen was sure you were taking shelter in the hut. She guessed it was snowing up there, and that you hadn't been able to get farther. But it really felt awful!'

'Up there! Mean to say it hasn't been snowing here?' demanded Jo, setting the Robin on her feet again.

'No. It's been rather grey; but there was no snow.'

By this time they were all in the *Gastzimmer* except Miss Stewart, who was seeing to the carrying of Miss Wilson to bed.

'Take your things off,' said Anne. 'You must all be dead, I should think.'

'No fear! It was rather tiring coming down, of course,

but we've had the sleigh ride from Neustift since then, and I'm not specially tired,' said Joey.

'Let's go and change,' suggested Ruth. 'I want a bath, too.'

'Me too!' put in Dorothy. 'I feel so sticky. But there wasn't any way of getting washed up there 'cept with snow-water, and Charlie wouldn't let us use that.'

They all made a bee-line for the door, through which Eustacia, not caring to join in the merry chatter, had gone some minutes ago. Up to their rooms they went, to be met by Frau Blitzen and the information that the fair little *Engländerin* had gone to take a bath. 'But I have boiled much water,' went on the good lady, beaming broadly at them. 'There will be enough for all.'

'I like her cheek!' murmured Jo, referring to Eustacia. She waited till the summons came for her to go to the tub, emerging ten minutes later, clean even to her hair, for she had given it a rubbing. Then back to her room to get into clean clothes. 'I hope *Abendessen* is ready,' she said anxiously. 'I'm famishing!'

The gong sounded for *Abendessen*, and, with one arm round Robin and the other through Anne's, she ran downstairs and into the *Gastzimmer*, where Eustacia was waiting for them with Miss Stewart, who looked like her jolly self once more.

'Robin is having *Abendessen* with us for once,' said Miss Stewart. 'After that, it must be bed for everyone. We are catching the nine o'clock train to Innsbruck tomorrow, and the next day we must go up to the Tiernsee. I should go on tomorrow, but I don't want to tire out the small fry, and we have to walk up from Spärtz, you know.'

They gathered round the table with beaming faces as Frau Blitzen served out bowlfuls of thick vegetable soup, with the little sausages they all liked so much.

'How is Miss Wilson?' asked Joey, before she began.

'Better, I think.'

'She won't be coming with us, will she?' queried Anne.

Miss Stewart shook her head. 'No; I'm afraid not. That's a nasty sprain, and she must rest her foot for another week at least. Luckily, there's quite a good doctor in this valley, and he's been sent for. I expect him directly, and then we shall know what we are to do.'

'If only you hadn't made such an ass of yourself,

Eustacia,' said Ruth, who was a very downright child, 'Miss Wilson would be all right.'

'What do you mean?' cried Eustacia, flaring up. 'How was it *my* fault?'

'Never mind now,' said Miss Stewart sharply. 'Go on with your soup, Ruth.—And Eustacia, don't play with yours. The rest of us are nearly finished.'

Choking down her anger, Eustacia finished her soup, and when large plates of *Rinderbraten*, or roast beef, with *Kartoffeln*, *Rotkohl*, and *Aprikosen*, were placed before them, she waded through hers in glum silence. The meal was rounded off with *Obstpastete* and, of course, coffee. By this time the Robin was nearly asleep, and Miss Stewart, seeing how drowsy they all were, ordered them off to bed without delay. They went without a murmur.

It was morning when they awoke, and the day was a grey one. Jo stretched herself, yawned, and then got up, and went to the window to look. 'It's snowing up there again, I'll bet,' she said cheerfully. 'The clouds are down again!'

'Well, thank goodness you aren't there yet, then,' replied Anne, joining her. 'I wonder how Bill is this morning.'

'If we get dressed, we might be able to find out,' suggested Jo, with a glance at the cot, where the Robin still slept peacefully.

'We'll have to be very quiet,' said Anne, following her gaze. 'The Robin ought to sleep for ages yet. She was up later than she ever is at school.'

They dressed in silence, always with an eye to the slumbering child, who never moved. Jo bent over her before they left the room, watching the little face, rosy with the sleep-flush. The long lashes never quivered, and the breath came softly and evenly from her parted lips.

They slipped along to the door of the room occupied by the two mistresses, and Joey scratched gently at it, till Miss Stewart appeared, ready dressed.

'Good morning. How is Miss Wilson?' asked Jo properly.

Miss Stewart smiled. 'Good morning, girls. Miss Wilson is much better this morning, I think. She is still drowsy, so I am leaving her to sleep again, if she will. How is the Robin?' she added anxiously.

'Still sleeping,' said Jo.

'Good!' replied Miss Stewart. 'I'll just peep in at her,

118

I think. You two go to the others first and tell them to be sure to be very quiet.'

They went, and met in the *Gastzimmer*, where the table was already set for *Frühstück*.

'I wonder how long the others will be?' said the mistress. 'I have begged Frau Blitzen to ring no bells, so when the coffee comes you two had better run upstairs and tell them.'

Anne nodded, and Joey added her assent too. 'How long will Miss Wilson have to stay here?' she asked.

'I don't quite know. Two or three weeks, at any rate. I wish you and Eustacia hadn't seen fit to quarrel, Joey. If it hadn't been for that silly child's actions this would not have occurred.'

'But the storm would have come, anyhow,' Anne reminded her, seeing that Joey had no mind to answer.

Miss Stewart sighed. 'I know that. The thing is that I really don't quite know what to do about leaving Miss Wilson. Here comes Frau Blitzen with the coffee, so run off you two, and warn the others.'

Most of the girls appeared at once; but Eustacia, who was stiff and sore from her gallivantings of the previous two days, had not yet got into her frock.

'Can I help you?' asked Anne, advancing.

'No!' snapped Eustacia. 'I'll look after myself, thank you.'

Anne went away with angry eyes. Really, Eustacia was past bearing! She didn't know that Eustacia was suffering, not only bodily discomfort, but also the pangs of conscience. *She* knew quite well that had she not been so silly about accepting Jo Bettany's proffered aid on the mountain-slope, the accident to 'Bill' would, in all probability, have never happened. 'But I'll never let them know I think so,' she decided. 'That horrid Jo would crow over me so! Oh! How I hate her—and all of them! But I'll make them suffer yet for all the unhappiness they've given me here!'

She opened her purse before she went down, and examined the little hoard of money therein; Eustacia was careful by nature. The careless spendings of most of the girls were never hers. She had bought but little since the beginning of term, and she had quite a nice sum in that purse of hers. She put it away, and then went slowly out of the room.

The others were all seated at the table, eating rolls and honey and drinking their coffee, when she arrived in the *Gastzimmer*, and Miss Stewart was obviously not too pleased at her late coming.

She said nothing beyond a chilly 'Good-morning' as the girl entered; but there was a spark in her blue eyes that told of a temper kept under control only by an effort. At the end of the meal Joey begged to be excused, and slipped off upstairs to see how the Robin was. She found the small girl rousing up, and ran downstairs again to beg a break-fast-tray for her. When she returned with it, the baby was wide-awake, and looked much as usual, though there were faint shadows under the dark eyes. However, Jo had not sufficient experience to detect them.

'*Grüss Gott, mein Liebling,*' she said, setting down her burden and kissing the small girl tenderly. 'Have you slept well, birdling?'

'Yes, thank you,' said the Robin. Then her eyes fell on the tray. 'Must I, Zoë? I am not hungry.'

'Oh, but see the pretty bowl of milk, and the little twisted rolls and the yellow butter,' said Jo persuasively. 'Try *one* roll, Robin—to please me. And a sip of the milk.'

She was soon satisfied, and lay back on her pillows, com-plaining that she felt tired.

Jo was alarmed. The Robin never had a big appetite, but she generally enjoyed her food; and this weariness was not like her at all. 'Lie back, darling,' she said tenderly. 'Can you go to sleep again?' She tucked the baby in and leaned over her. Already the black lashes were lying on the cheeks that struck Joey as being paler than usual. With a hideous dread in her heart the elder child stole out of the room and downstairs to Miss Stewart.

'How is Robin, Joey?' asked the mistress anxiously.

'I don't know,' said Joey slowly. 'She—she isn't quite —herself, Miss Stewart.'

Miss Stewart jumped up from her seat and hurried upstairs without a word. The girls gathered round Jo.

'What is it, Jo?' asked Anne fearfully. 'I thought she looked as usual when we were dressing.'

'She seems dead tired,' replied Jo curtly. 'She didn't want her breakfast, and she went to sleep again at once. She looks rather white, too,' she ended with a gulp.

'Naturally,' observed Eustacia. 'She was up far too late last night—delicate child as you always say she is.'

Jo swung round on her. 'Hold your tongue!' she snarled. '*You're* the cause of all this! If you hadn't made such an ass of yourself on the mountain-side, Bill would have been all right. We shouldn't have had to wait for an ambulance to bring her down, and we'd have been here hours before we were. As it is, the Robin had to fret all that time, and if she's ill, *you* are to blame for it!'

Miss Stewart returned at that moment, so any further talk was out of the question. She shook her head at the girls, and then turned to Jo. 'She is desperately tired, Jo. There can be no doubt of that. All the worry of waiting has told on her badly, and she is not a strong child. But I honestly believe that it is nothing else. She is sleeping quite naturally, and she is cool, and her pulse seems normal. However, the doctor from Neustift will be coming presently to see Miss Wilson's ankle, and I will ask him to look at her when he comes. He may think she ought to stay where she is for a day or two. In that case, I shall wire Madame, and ask if you may stay with her. Miss Wilson certainly can't be moved for a week or two. She broke one of the little bones in the foot when she fell, and must lie up for the present.' Her eyes went to Eustacia, and she added, 'Oh, Eustacia! If only you had learned self-control, all this need never have happened.'

For once, Eustacia had nothing to say in her own defence, and there was silence.

At twelve o'clock the doctor came, and, after he had finished with 'Bill', he came to the baby, who was awake by this time and more like herself. He examined her carefully, and then gave it as his opinion that she should stay where she was till the morrow. Then, he thought they should take her to Innsbruck, and, the following day, to Spärtz. After a day spent in the little town at the foot of the mountains, they might carry her up to the Tiern valley, and so straight on to the Sonnalpe, where, he thought, she ought to spend the next weeks under the immediate charge of her own doctor.

Miss Stewart arranged to take the other girls to Innsbruck at once, where they would be met by Herr Marani, who had undertaken to see them safely to Briesau. She herself would return on the last train to Fulpmes, and, with Jo, would bring the Robin to Innsbruck on the morrow. They would go to the Maranis, and Herr Marani would help Joey with the Robin for the rest of the journey, while she herself returned once more to make final arrangements for 'Bill', who must stay where she was for a week or two, to give the injured bone a chance of knitting.

The Saturday saw the Robin safely at the Sonnalpe, and Joey back at school. Miss Stewart came up on the Sunday, having left Miss Wilson resigned to her fate, and school settled down once more. But that little action of Eustacia's had made a change. It was the summer-term before the school baby returned to her place in the school, and even then she had to be carefully watched, for the strain on her baby nerves had thrown her back more than a year, as Dr. Jem said savagely when he was discussing it with Mademoiselle and Madge. Joey hated Eustacia with a force and tenacity that was startlingly unlike her. And Eustacia herself, shunned by the rest for what she had done, even though it had been unintentional so far as 'Bill's' accident was concerned, daily became more and more bitter and more and more intent on gaining her 'revenge'.

Chapter XX

OSTRACISED

EUSTACIA knew quite well that most of the girls did not like her. That this was something to be regretted never dawned on her. She still held herself to be far above the majority of them in every way. At the same time she was conscious that she held a feeble affection for Evadne, who had shown her sundry kindnesses. And she was not indifferent to Elsie and Ilonka and one or two others of the same set. But there was no friendliness to be encountered from any of them now. The juniors who had been with that ill-fated expedition to the Stubai took no pains to hide from the others what had happened, and it lost nothing in the telling. Ruth, in particular, nearly turned it into a penny dreadful, and Jo got a shock when Amy Stevens came to ask if it was true that Eustacia had tried to push her down a crevasse, and then had followed suit with 'Bill', while the others had only been able to save the pair of them by forming a long chain and hauling steadily, and the Robin screamed for help till someone came rushing and caught back the vengeful Eustacia by the ankles, so that she was dragged away!

'The Robin wasn't there, as I should think your own sense might have told you!' snapped Jo, when she had recovered her breath after listening to this amazing recital. 'And we weren't near any crevasse—we only looked at the glacier. And tell whoever told you to stop telling lies, or she'll come to a bad end!' With this she stalked away, leaving Amy staring after her.

'Of course Ruth exaggerated—little ninny!' said Margia, when her small sister came to tell her about it. 'If you'd thought, you'd have *known* that they wouldn't let the Robin go climbing like that. As for what really happened, Eustacia pushed Joey away when she came to help her, and jerked Bill off her feet doing it. That made them all hours later in getting down than they would have been, and the Robin was fretting about Jo—naturally—and it's upset her. That's all that happened, and you'd better stick to that. I know, 'cos Louise told me.'

Amy went away to retail this to her own clan, and they one and all made up their minds to have nothing whatsoever to do with the girl who had caused all the trouble.

The Fourth and Fifth, meanwhile, had decided to follow the same tactics as the Third, and Eustacia found herself in splendid isolation. She had a most uncomfortable interview with Mademoiselle, in which that lady forgot her usual gentleness, and pointed out uncompromisingly what mischief she had accomplished. It was a rare thing for Mademoiselle to be stern, but on this occasion not even that iron disciplinarian, Madge Russell, could have bettered her, and Eustacia was half-scared by her severity. The staff, hearing all that Miss Stewart had to tell them, were disapproving in their attitude, and though no one directly alluded to the affair, Eustacia felt they were blaming her for the trouble about the Robin, Miss Wilson's accident, and the extra work that had fallen on their own shoulders in consequence.

Joey, sent for by a staff meeting to explain what she had

done to make Eustacia so dislike her, had very little to say. 'I have called her a silly ass sometimes,' she said, 'and so she *is*! I've squelched her for telling tales—and, of course, there was that library——' She stopped short, nearly biting her tongue in her sudden remembrance of the fact that not a mistress in the place knew anything about that affair, and stood, scarlet and embarrassed, before them.

'What about the library, Jo?' demanded Miss Annersley.

'Nothing,' mumbled Jo.

Miss Annersley fixed her with a cold grey eye. 'That is rubbish!' she declared. 'Have you had any trouble with Eustacia over the library rules?'

Jo looked round desperately in search of inspiration, but found none. 'Ye-es,' she acknowledged reluctantly at length.

'What happened?'

'Just—just—she was reading there when she oughtened.'

' "Ought not," ' corrected the English mistress. 'Am I to understand that she has been dealt with?'

'Yes; Mary called a prefects' meeting, and we had her up,' said Joe relievedly.

'And you think she bears a grudge against you for the punishment you inflicted then?'

'I s'pose so. She—she doesn't look on things as *we* do, Miss Annersley,' said Jo earnestly.

'I know that,' said Miss Annersley. 'And that is all you can tell me?'

'*Yes*,' said Jo fervently.

She was dismissed after that, and the staff congregated together to discuss the matter.

'It seems absurdly little to have caused all this trouble, said Miss Nalder.

'I know. But girls are like that,' Miss Annersley pointed out, and they were obliged to leave matters as they stood. Meanwhile, they were all pledged to keep a keen watch for any further developments. However, nothing of any interest occurred for the next week or two, for Jo was busy with the *Chaletian*, and Eustacia was engaged in perfecting her plans for her great revenge.

Guides and school-work and folk-dancing filled up the time for most of the girls, and Eustacia and her doings soon ceased to be the centre of interest when Mary called the School together to demand that they should get on with their preparations for the end-of-term sale of work.

'The sale is only three weeks off, so I want to know what you intend to do about it.'

'Nothing till I get the mag off to the printers!' declared Jo. 'I'm up to my eyes in it, and till it's done I can't take on a single other job!'

'Well—you've some excuse,' acknowledged Mary grudgingly. 'All the same, I wish you'd hurry up and get it away.'

No one else had any excuse worth hearing, as the head-girl remarked, so they were all ordered to devote any spare time they might have to producing articles for the sale, and for the next few days everyone was too busy to think of anything but work.

Jo devoted a good half of her prep-time to the magazine, and, when the end of the week came, announced with a deep sigh of relief that it had gone to the printers

Gifts began to come in from the old girls too, and the staff brought their offerings.

'It's not too bad,' said Mary, when she had set out everything that had come in and called the School to view them. 'Mademoiselle is going to make us a lot of cakes and sweets, and Charlie is knitting stockings as hard as she can. They will always sell here—and hers are so jolly.'

'Wanda is sending us china as usual,' added Marie von Eschenau; 'and Friedel is carving some wooden boxes in his spare time.'

'Then, there's Bernie's baby-frocks to come,' said Jo.

'And she also said that she was sending some peasant lace from Lyons,' put in Frieda.

'We simply *can't* be beaten by the Saints!' said Mary.

'I call that a most un-Christian sentiment,' said a prim voice from the middle seat.

As if Eustacia had not spoken, Mary went on: 'Remember, we have our bed to settle in the children's ward at the Sanatorium, and this year I should so like it if we could manage a second one. Our subs won't run to it alone; but if we can clear an extra lot at the sale, we might just manage it. I had a letter from Grizel yesterday, enclosing her subscription for the year—and she's doubled it. Also, that girl, Gerry Challoner, she brought with her at the end of last term, has sent us twenty pounds. She's Grizel's friend, so I'm going to accept it. Bernhilda and Kurt have sent us a big sub too; and Wanda and Friedel have done the same. But it means more than that to do what I want, and we must all buckle to and work like niggers for the rest of the time.' Mary sat down, and the girls cheered her hilariously.

Joey got up next. 'I've been too busy with the mag to do much lately,' she began, 'but I do agree with Mary, and I know we all do. Let's work as hard as we can, and see if we can't do as she wishes. I think it would be great!'

Deira had a few words to add. 'This is my last term,' she said soberly. 'It's Mary's too. If we could go away remembering that we'd managed to get two beds, it would be the best memory of the Chalet School we could have.'

The School rose at this, and vowed its intention of out-doing itself. That second bed should be assured to the sanatorium if it could be done. Eustacia listened, with her lips compressed and her face grim. She, for one, would have neither part nor lot in this affair. Let the others work for their silly beds if they liked! She would have nothing to do with it!

When the girls streamed away to their various pursuits she remained behind, industriously reading the book she had brought with her.

The work went on steadily all the evening till the supper-bell rang and they had to put away their work. Eustacia closed her book, strolled over to her private locker, and put it away. Later, when she came to think it over, she couldn't remember a single word of what she had read. She went in to supper with a superior smile on her lips, and sat down in her usual seat between Ilonka Barkocz and Suzanne Mercier. At once Ilonka moved her seat a little farther away, and Suzanne followed her example. In spite of herself, Eustacia flushed at the actions of the two; but she said nothing. Instead, she helped herself to another piece of the rye-bread she cordially detested, but which the girls always had for supper. Then she glanced down at her plate. An untouched piece lay there already. She glanced round. Margia had done that very same thing only the week before half-term exeat, and had been instantly subjected to a volley of teasing. Eustacia expected the same, but no one seemed to have seen it.

She wanted the salt, and turned to ask someone to pass it to her, but before she could say anything Joey Bettany, who was at the head of the table, had seen her want, and called down to Ilonka to pass it to her. Ilonka promptly set it before her without looking at her, and then went on with her conversation with Cornelia Flower. The same thing happened when she wanted more milk. Paula von Rothenfels bade Suzanne pass up Eustacia's glass, and Suzanne passed it and then handed it back, her eyes glued to the table.

After supper the middles went off to bed, and in the Violet dormitory Greta McDonald and Cornelia Flower chatted gaily to each other as usual while they undressed. When they were ready for bed both knelt and said their prayers, and then climbed in—Eustacia could hear them.

'Night-night, Greta!' called Cornelia cheerfully. 'Sweet dreams!'

'Good-night, Corney!' responded Greta.

Eustacia finished her own preparation and climbed in between the sheets.

'Good-night,' she said in her most stilted tones.

No reply came from either cubicle. She might never have spoken. A little later came light footsteps down the corridor, and then a prefect, Marie von Eschenau, enter the room to see that everyting was as it should be. 'Good-night, Cornelia,' she said gaily. 'Good-night, Greta.' Then in chilly tones, 'Good-night, Eustacia'. She switched off the lights, and was gone.

Cornelia and Greta settled themselves for slumber, and presently Eustacia could hear their even breathing, telling that they were safely off. She herself could not sleep. She lay watching the slip of window she could see through the chink Marie had left in her curtains. Quiet sounds floated up from downstairs, where the seniors still had an hour's grace. The footsteps of the servants, coming up to go to bed, since theirs was an early beginning, came to her. Later, she heard the elder girls racing softly up the stairs, mindful of the fact that the middles would all be sleeping by this time. Overhead came the sound of their tread, then it was muffled as they changed into bedroom slippers. Doors opened and shut softly; she could hear snatches of conversation. Even these ceased after a time, and she realised that the seniors were all in bed too, and sleeping like Greta and Cornelia.

A long time seemed to pass before she heard sounds betokening the departure of the staff bedwards. Then came the sound of Miss Stewart's soft Highland accents, and Miss Annersley's deeper notes replying. Their doors closed; a few sounds drifted to her ears; then these, too, ended, and the Chalet was quiet.

Downstairs the clock boomed eleven strokes—it was an old grandfather which Madge had brought with her from England, and its sweet bell-notes reminded the unhappy child of one which stood in the hall of her father's house in that quiet street in Oxford. Oh, if only she were there!

By and by there came other footsteps, and the sound of the doors opening, and then closing very softly. Eustacia knew, for Evadne had once told her, that this was Mademoiselle, going the rounds before she retired. Every night she entered the dormitories to assure herself that all was well. Any girl waking because of toothache or a bad dream might know that about this time a faint subdued light would shine in the room for a minute, and the kindly Head of the School would be at her side at the faintest murmur. Eustacia knew now that she had only to whisper 'Mademoiselle!' and Mademoiselle would be with her, and would listen patiently to anything she might have to say. If only she could overcome the dumb devil of pride that was having its own way with her just now, and say she was sorry and would try to do better, Eustacia knew that much of her trouble would be at an end. She had often thought how nice it would be if the girls would leave her alone, but she had had no idea that it would feel so terrible to be set outside their affairs. She wanted to say she was sorry; she wanted to cry about it to someone, and then forget it all. But—no one had ever heard such words from the lips of Eustacia Benson. No one had ever seen her cry because she was unhappy over her own wrong-doing. And even as she struggled the door opened and Mademoiselle came in. She peeped into the other two cubicles, and was evidently satisfied. She was coming to Eustacia's now, and now was Eustacia's time. 'Go on! Tell her!' whispered her better self. But the other side mocked at the bare idea. What! *She* acknowledge that she had been wrong? Never! And the good angels turned sadly away as Eustacia closed her eyes and lay motionless when her curtains were softly parted and Mademoiselle looked at her.

Mademoiselle stood there a long time it seemed. Eustacia, lying with her eyes shut tightly, wondered if she would ever go. Then there came to her ears a low-spoken, *'Pauvre petite!'* the curtains fell again, and she could hear the Head softly leave the room and close the door behind her.

Once she was certain that she was safe from interference, Eustacia turned on her side, buried her face in the pillows, and cried as she had never cried in all her life before. But the good moment had passed, not to return till much water had flowed under the bridge, and when the morning came Eustacia was her ordinary smug self again; and so she remained until the terrible happening put an end to all feuds and all hates, and a new Eustacia Benson was born who had very little in common with the old one.

Chapter XXI

ACCIDENTS

'INK—ink! Margia, aren't you ink-monitress? Then why on earth can't you do your duty properly?' Louise Redmond waved an empty ink-well at Margia, her face flushed with righteous indignation.

Margia stared at her.

'Where's—my—ink? Oh, you Britishers!' repeated Louise scornfully.

'And what price mine?' demanded Anne plaintively.

'And mine?' added Paula von Rothenfels.

Margia gasped. 'But I filled *all* the ink-wells first thing this morning!' she protested.

'Are you certain that you don't mean that you emptied them?' asked Yvette Mercier, elder sister of Suzanne. 'For, see—there is no ink in mine, either.'

Margia made for her own desk. 'Mine's gone too!' she cried, after investigating; and sat down limply.

'But what has happened?' Giovanna Donati desired to know.

'It's those wretched infants in the Fourth!' said Margia furiously. 'I had a row with Evvy yesterday because she had the cool cheek to take my book without asking me. They know I'm inker this term, of course; so they've

129

planned this. Oh, when I get hold of Evvy!' Judging from
her expression, Evadne would get off lightly if she were
boiled in oil.

The rest plunged in the direction of the ink-can, which
should have been half-full.

'Not a drop left!' cried Louise, as she grabbed it.

'What those children need is slapping.' Paula gave vent
to this profound utterance with a vigour which told that
she was well aroused.

'I dare say!' Margia got up from her seat, and took the
ink-can from Louise. 'Unfortunately, we can't quite do it.'
She marched off to find Deira O'Hagan, who was stationery-
prefect this term, in order to demand more ink from her.

The rest, brought to a standstill in their work till the
ink should come, formed a group in the middle of the
room to discuss the iniquities of the Fourth.

'Evvy's at the bottom of it, of course,' said Louise. 'I've
only been here a term, but it doesn't take long to know
who's the leader of *those* folk!'

'But it is cheek to treat our ink-wells like this!' said
Paula hotly. 'Even if Evadne has quarrelled with Margia,
she has no right to empty *our* ink-wells!'

'Oh, Paula! Can't you understand?' cried Giovanna.
'They have done this so that we may be enraged with
Margia.'

'I could ring their silly little necks!' cried Louise.

'We must—how do you say it?—get even with them,'
declared Paula.

'True enough; but what shall we do?'

The Fifth became silent while they thought.

'It *must* be something *good*!' said Louise at last. 'I can't
think of anything out of the way.—Can anyone else?'

Margia returned at this moment with the ink-can, her
face very flushed and her eyes angry. Deira busy herself,
had not been pleased at being summoned to the stationery
cupboard out of hours, and she had scolded Margia sharply
for not coming before. Explanations were impossible, as
Margia had no wish to embroil the Fourth with the prefects,
so she had been obliged to listen with apparent meekness
to Deira's fulminations, and was nearly boiling over in
consequence. She filled up the ink-wells, and set the can
down in a corner, all in ominous silence, and the others
watched her in equal silence. 'Better get on with prep now,'

she said, as she went to wash her hands. 'We'll discuss this later.'

Once prep was over, the Fifth discussed reprisals with vim and point. The worst of it was that they could think of nothing which seemed to meet the case adequately. Apple-pie beds were rejected scornfully. So was the suggestion that the Fourth's desks should be closed with cobbler's wax.

'We might stitch them into their cubicles,' said Paula, with recollections of a prank played on some of them by former seniors two years before.

But Margia would have none of it. 'Let's be original if we can, for goodness' sake!' she cried.

The word 'stitch' had given Anne an idea. 'Matey is awfully down on untidiness, isn't she?' she queried.

The rest turned and regarded her amazedly.

'Doesn't she inspect the middles every morning to see that no buttons and hooks are missing?' went on Anne.

Margia's eyes gleamed at this. She was beginning to get Anne's idea. 'Yes; she does. Well I know it! The hours of free time I've had to spend doing mending that *I* didn't think was necessary, but *she* did, would fill up a year, I should think!'

'Explain!' implored the others; so Anne explained.

'It would be an excellent idea for each one of the Fourth to have a button loose—or nearly so—tomorrow. Or there might be other things. The cat is very fond of lying on blazers, and she seems to spend all her spare time casting her coat. You know what Matey says about hairy blazers!'

They had got the idea at last, and promptly went wild with joy.

'But it is a splendid idea, my Anne!' vowed Yvette.

'They will be very busy in their spare time,' added Paula. 'Yes; I like it.'

'How are we going to manage it?' asked Sophie Hemel, a quiet girl, who rarely talked much.

'Wait till they have gone to bed, of course. Then we'll go to the cloaker, and settle them. I don't *think*,' added Anne pensively, 'that they will meddle with our ink-can again.'

When *Abendessen* was over, the Fourth went off to bed, and once they were safely out of the way the Fifth retired to their form-room till they knew that the Sixth were busy

131

with their own affairs, and unlikely to trouble about them.

'Come on, now,' said Margia, at length, nearly dancing with excitement. 'I've got to go in about ten minutes, and I simply *must* have a hand in this!'

'We can't all go at once,' said Louise with common-sense. 'The Sixth or the staff would be sure to hear us and come to see what we were doing. You and Paula and Anne pop along first—oh, and Yvette and Signa, as they go to bed with you.'

They slipped out at once. Margia, Signa, and Yvette, although members of the Fifth, were not yet fifteen, so ranked as middles for the present. However, in considera-tion of their attainments, they were given a extra half-hour before bedtime, and this had nearly expired. During the ten minutes left to them they managed to do a fair amount of mischief, however. Margia removed a button from Evadne's coat and also snapped one of her boot-laces. Signa removed all the buttons from Cornelia's blazer, dropping them into the pocket, and Yvette bore off those of Elsie, Ilonka, and Suzanne, to wipe them round the cat's bed, whence she returned them to their pegs, liberally adorned with long white hairs. Then they retired to bed, and Anne and Paula finished their work, and then returned to the form-room, where they settled down with bazaar-work, while three others slipped out to do what they could for the Fourth.

'You're awfully quiet, you people,' observed Joey, as she entered the room a little later. 'What *are* you doing? And why don't you join us in the common-room?'

'Too busy,' said Anne.

Joey went the rounds, admired their work and then left them.

The sequel came next morning, when five middles turned up at *Frühstück* in blazers that, as Mary said, literally *sprouted* cat's hairs, and Cornelia was forced to put on a jersey, since *her* blazer was minus all its buttons.

Matron glared at the six, and summoned them to her after breakfast, to demand the reason for their untidiness. 'You are disgraceful!' she snapped at them. 'Go to your rooms, and brush all those cat's hairs off at once, you five. —As for you, Cornelia, you may spend your free time after *Mittagessen* in sewing on those buttons. I hope you haven't lost any?'

'They—they're all in my pocket,' stammered Cornelia, who was nearly choking with rage.

When it came to the walk, and Evadne found that, in addition to having to sew on a button, she had also to knot her boot-lace—thereby earning a smart rebuke from Matron—the wrath of the Fourth-form leader was unspeakable. Sundry other people felt the same way, and it is a fact that most of the Fourth had to give up their reading-time to mending. Only Eustacia of them all had escaped from some retribution, and, strange to state, she resented this even more fiercely than she would have done had she shared with the rest.

As for Matron, she was furious, and, fearing an outbreak of carelessness on the part of the entire Middle School, she called them all to her sanctum and rated them soundly on the iniquities of missing buttons, hairy blazers, and broken boot-laces.'

There was nothing to be done about it, of course. The furious middles had no explanation they could offer. And though they were certain that the Fifth had been at work, they had no proof of it, and, even if they had, they would have scorned to say anything.

That was the beginning of a week in which everything seemed to go wrong. On the Wednesday Mary Burnett, climbing up to lift down some models for model drawing, slipped and fell, clutching at the map-rack which was near, and bringing that down with her. The maps fell in every direction, and Joey and Frieda, happening to catch at the same one, managed to tear it across between them. What 'Bill's' horror would be when she should return and see her precious map in two halves the pair did not like to think. As it was, they had to endure a sharp scolding from 'Charlie', who was seeing to their geography at present, and who made herself exceedingly unpleasant about it. Mary had bumped her funny bone and bitten her tongue badly in her fall, and the model lay in three pieces, and was no further good to anybody.

At *Kaffee und Kuchen* Deira, absent-mindedly turning on the tap of the urn, deluged the tray, the table and the floor with coffee.

A pillow-fight took place that night between the inhabitants of the Amber and Yellow dormitories, and an electric bulb was smashed, and Amy Stevens slipped and fell, banging her head against the leg of a bed. Matron, summoned to the scene by the noise, gave them all short-shrift. She made them tidy up the rooms, and sent Elsie Carr downstairs for a brush and dust-pan to remove the bits of broken glass from the floor. Then she applied something to the rapidly swelling bump on Amy's head, telling her severely that it was her own fault and served her right. After that she waited between the rooms till they were all safely in bed, and finally condemned them to silence in the bedrooms for the next week.

Thursday was ushered in with a shriek from Joey Bettany when she jumped out of bed onto her hair-brush, which she had flung down the night before without bothering to see that it fell on the bureau. The rest of the day was 'Jonah' day, for nothing went right. In the Third, Kitty Burnett carelessly spilt water over the black-board chalk, and had to be sent to rout Deira out from a history lesson for more. The Fourth seemed to have got up with little black dogs on every shoulder, and, before the morning was half over, most of them were embroiled in a quarrel with one or another. The Fifth had been careless in a previous French lesson, and had, without a single exception, done the wrong preparation, much to the annoyance of Mademoiselle Lachenais, who forgot her usual smiling calm and sentenced them to doing the correct work in addition to their normal prep for the next lesson.

As for the Sixth, they were too great to be troubled over little matters, but Jo, who had expected a letter from Madge that morning and been disappointed of it, went about like a thunder-cloud, and snapped at Mary till even that placid person took herself off, vowing that she would have nothing further to do with anyone so bad-tempered. Simone had a crying fit over her geometry, and was sent out of the room by Miss Leslie till she could 'remember to be a prefect, and not a silly cry-baby!'—a criticism that wounded her deeply. Frieda, Bianca, Marie, Carla, and a new girl, Arda von de Windt, all made a dive for the same biscuit at break, and contrived to upset and smash the plate between them. And Natash Pokrovska and Deira O'Hagan, both bending down suddenly to pick up Deira's fountain-pen, which had fallen from her desk, banged their heads smartly together, so that they saw stars for a few moments, and the tears poured down their cheeks.

Nor was that the worst. Jem came down from the Son-nalpe to say that Jo must postpone her expected visit at the week-end, as the Robin had been poorly all the week, and he thought the excitement of having her beloved Jo with her would upset her. 'You can come next week,' he said soothingly.

'Oh no, I can't!' snapped Jo, who was grievously disappointed. 'You know as well as I do that the sale is next Saturday! Do have a little common-sense!'

'That's not the way to speak to anyone,' he said, when he had recovered from his surprise at being addressed in this way. 'You ought to be ashamed of yourself!'

'Well, I'm not! And tell Madge I was rude to you—do!' retorted Jo, who was feeling at odds with all the world and didn't care who knew it.

He looked at her speculatively, but said no more—to her. But when the afternoon came Joey found herself condemned to bed while the others went for a long and splashy walk. March had come with unusual warmth, and the snow was melting quickly. It was not pleasant walking, but just because she couldn't go, Joey grumbled and growled, and made herself as unpleasant as possible. Stalking upstairs to bed, she nearly fell over Eustacia, who had been stopping down to pull up her stocking. 'Why can't you look where you're going?' she demanded.

'It is *you* who did not look where you were going,' replied Eustacia with perfect truth.

'Well, what do you want to stop on the stairs to do that for? You ought to see that your stockings are all right before you leave your dormitory!' snapped Jo with equal truth.

Eustacia lost her temper, and answered Jo as rudely as she could, and the quarrel might have gone on for an hour had not Matron, overhearing them from her room, come to investigate. She made quick work of them, ordering off Eustacia to the walk and Jo to bed.

But that squabble had put the last touch to Eustacia's decision, and she finally made up her mind to do as she had thought of doing ever since half-term. It would be a splendid revenge, for it *must* hurt the School. She would write a note saying that it was mainly owing to Joey Bettany that she had done this; and they would have a bad time of it until they got news of her.

135

In other words, the silly child had decided to run away to England. She had plenty of money and any amount of assurance. The chances are that, had everything remained as it was that afternoon, she would have carried out her plan so far as reaching England and Oxford was concerned. She had decided to go there; and there is no doubt that such a thing might have caused the Chalet School harm in England.

But Eustacia reckoned without the weather and the thaw. These two factors made just the difference, and the lesson she had to learn came through them.

Chapter XXII

THE BEGINNING OF IT

FRIDAY came, and brought with it various troubles. Among other things, Jo woke up with a touch of toothache. She had known for some time that one of her teeth needed attention, but a dread of the dentist had made her keep it secret; now she was to suffer for that secrecy. Throughout the morning the pain grew and grew. Gradually her cheek swelled, till it was impossible to avoid notice, and when the bell rang for the end of lessons she was seized on by Matron, who desired to know what was wrong.

'It's a bad tooth,' mumbled Jo.

'How do you know?' demanded Matron.

'Hole in it.' Talking hurt, so Jo made her speeches as short as possible.

Matron marched her off to the sick-room, and made her open her mouth as wide as she could—which was not very wide. 'Bad tooth?' she snapped, when her inspection was over. 'I should think so! Why didn't you speak about it before?'

'Don't know.'

'You must go to Innsbruck tomorrow if it's possible. You can stay here for the rest of today, and we'll try to reduce that swelling so that the dentist can get at it. It will have to come out, I expect—it doesn't look to me as though there were anything to stop. I'll tell Luise to make you a basin of bread and milk, and I'll mix you a lotion to hold in your mouth afterwards. Don't swallow any if you can help it—I don't want to have you sick into the bargain!'

An appointment had been made with the dentist for the next day, and Matron had taken advantage of it to go the rounds and select fifteen victims who all stood in more or less need of dental attention. Miss Stewart and Miss Annersley were to accompany them to Innsbruck, as they would be such a large party, and they would not return till the Sunday.

Miss Wilson had been brought back to school the previous day. The bone in her foot was knitting up well, but she was pale from the confinement and pain she had suffered, and was very glad to get back to Briesau, though she said no one could have been kinder than Frau Blitzen. Walking was forbidden for the present, but Dr. Jem had sent down a wheel-chair for her, and she would sit in that, and so be able to take her classes as usual.

With the pain in her face greatly improved, and her swollen cheek reduced almost to its normal size, Joey got permission from Matron to sit with the mistress in the evening, and they spent a pleasant hour together, discussing the Stubai and their adventures. No mention was made of the Robin. Bill' knew better than that. Also, she steered clear of the topic of Eustacia. Matron came in at half-past seven and ordered both her patients off to bed. The morrow's expedition meant an early start, and Jo was not strong.

They were up at half-past six and on their way by eight o'clock. They had to reach Spärtz in time for the ten to ten train from Kufstein and, though the snow was melting, it would not be an easy walk.

Jo joined the others resignedly. With them were Mary, Frieda, and Margia. Mary had a loose stopping; two of Frieda's teeth needed drilling; and Margia's biggest back tooth showed signs of needing attention. One of the juniors was to be fitted with a straightening bar, as her second teeth seemed inclined to project. They reached Innsbruck safely, to find the streets wallowing in mud, and everyone who could do so driving. Miss Annersley took two big taxis, and they were driven to Wilten, where Herr von Francius dwelt. Joey, as the worst of the bunch, was the first to enter the surgery, and he soon made an examination. 'It must come out, I fear,' he said at length, putting down his little steel mirror. 'I will, however, give you an injection which will kill all the pain. Be of courage; it will be over in a moment, and you will never feel him at all.'

'Thank you,' said Jo dubiously.

She sat quite still while he injected his mixture, and then, when he considered that it had had long enough to affect the part, he produced his forceps, clapped her head to his chest with a grip of iron, bade her open her mouth, and—there was a sudden jerk, and he was smiling at her, the big tooth held securely in front of her that she might see it, and it was practically over. Jo washed her mouth with some mixture he gave her, wiped her face with her handkerchief, and then rose up. 'Well, it's gone, anyhow,' she said in German.

He smiled on her. 'And a good thing too, *mein Fräulein*. Such a thing in your mouth was a poison-trap. The bleeding has ceased? Excellent! Now, permit that I assist you with your wraps, and then we will see the next patient.'

Jo got into her coat and beret, and went out, to send in Frieda, who was to come next. Mademoiselle had rung up the Mensches to tell them that Frieda would be in Innsbruck till Sunday afternoon, and they had promptly asked that she might go home once the tooth had been dealt with. Frieda, on hearing this, had asked that Jo might go with her; so Mademoiselle had arranged that they should be attended to first, and then they would be ready for Tante Luise, who would come to Herr von Francius's to chaperon them to Mariahilf.

Herr von Francius was a rapid worker. Before long, Frieda came out, and sent Mary in to him, and then she and Joey bade the others 'Good-bye' till the morrow, and ran off down the stairs to the street, where Tante Luise was awaiting them in a *droschke*. They climbed in, and were soon whirled away over the river, which was free once more, and whirling madly down to join the Danube.

Of that day there is no need to say much. They had *Mittagessen* in the Mariahilf-Strasse, and in the afternoon they sat quietly round the stove and talked of school news. In the evening they had music, and went to bed early, for both felt tired.

On the Sunday they went to the Hofkirche in the morning to hear High Mass, and in the afternoon Herr Mensch took them to the station, where they met the others, and all returned to Spärtz.

'We had a gorgeous time,' said Mary, when they had started. 'We went to the theatre in the evening, and saw *Die Fledermaus*. It is so pretty, and the music is delightful.'

'And in the afternoon we went to the Museum,' put in Margia. 'Charlie was with us, as Miss Annersley had the babes, and she was awfully decent about letting us see everything. We had a gorgeous meal in the Mariatheresien Strasse—*you* know the place! The one got up to look like a wine-cellar. This morning some of us went to service at the Europe, and the R.C.'s went to Mass somewhere or other. What did you do?'

'We were quite quiet and peaceful at home all the time,' said Jo calmly. 'We went to High Mass at the Hofkirche this morning, though.'

'O, that's where you were!' said Mary. 'I rather thought you might turn up at the Europe.'

'Didn't think of it,' replied Jo. 'And, anyhow, I wouldn't have missed the music at the Hofkirche for anything! It was wonderful!'

They had reached Hall, famed for its saltmines, by this time, and so were half-way to Spärtz. Jo, who had been chattering gaily all the way along—'to make up for lost time,' she said—suddenly fell silent, and said no more.

'What's up?' demanded Mary.

Jo shook herself. 'I don't know. I've a queer feeling that something's going wrong.'

'Rubbish!' said Mary. 'What could?'

'D'you mean a train accident?' asked Margia, with bated breath.

'Of course not! It's not that kind of feel at all. It's something to do with the others. Something's happened while we've been away.' She relapsed into silence again, her dread showing in her eyes; and the others guessed what her fears were.

Mary slipped a hand through her arm. 'I don't believe it's the Robin, Jo,' she said. 'Dr. Jem knew you were going with Frieda, didn't he? Then they'd have rung you up there or wired you or something, if it were that.'

There was common-sense in this, and Joey acknowledged

139

it. But her fears did not diminish, and the rest couldn't help her.

'It's far more likely to be Eustacia getting someone else into a mess,' declared Margia uncharitably. 'I'd believe anything of her!'

Jo said nothing, but her face wore a strained look, which did not vanish as the houses of Spärtz came in sight. When the train drew up near the platform she was the first to jump out, and she looked round nervously, as if she feared to find some messenger of woe awaiting them there. There was no one, however, so she turned away, looking relieved, and helped the little ones down the steep steps.

'We'll go to the Alte Toleranz for coffee,' decided Miss Annersley. 'Then, we'll call at Herr Anserl's for lanterns before we set off. We've plenty of time—it's only sixteen o'clock now.'

They streamed after her down the twisting street, and presently arrived at the Alte Toleranz, a plain whitewashed house, where lights were streaming from the lower windows on to the muddy pathway. It was quite evident that it had been raining heavily for some hours, and though it was fine now, Miss Annersley felt anxious. She did not want to be caught in a rainstorm half-way up the mountain-side. The trains were not running yet, nor would be for another month. They generally began with May, and this was only the end of March. They would have to walk every step of the way till they reached Seespitz, at any rate. Miss Annersley withdrew her gaze from the cloudy skies and directed it at Joey. The girl had so nearly died the previous term that they were all anxious about her. If there were any fear of rain, Miss Annersley knew that she must wait till it had cleared. They dared not risk any chills.

While the girls were drinking their coffee and eating their rolls she held counsel with the inn-keeper. He told her that it had poured all the previous day and all the night. With the coming of the dawn the rain had ceased to fall, and he thought it would hold off till night. After that, he expected it would come again.

'Could we reach the Tierntal before it comes, do you think?' asked Miss Annersley.

He considered. 'Which way go you, *gnädiges Fräulein*?'

'By the saw-mill,' replied Miss Annersley. 'It is nearest for us.'

'Then—yes; I think it possible. But you must hasten with your *Kaffee und Brötchen*.'

Miss Annersley did not want to stay in Spärtz. For one thing, if it began to rain again it might continue for days. It frequently did so at this time of the year. Also, she was anxious to get back to school. Like Jo, she had a feeling of impending disaster, and she wanted to be able to laugh at her own vague fears. She summoned 'Charlie' from the table, told her what the man had said, and asked her opinion.

'Go, by all means,' said the younger mistress. 'The girls have nearly finished. I'll hurry them up, and we can set out almost at once. You come and have some coffee, or you'll be dead tired by the time we get back. I'll try to get Herr Anserl on the phone, and ask him to meet us at the foot of the path with the lanterns. That will be best, I think.'

Miss Annersley agreed to this plan, and while she made a hasty meal, Miss Stewart contrived to get the eccentric music-master on the phone, and to make him understand what she wanted. He bawled back that he would meet them at the mill-stream, and then rang off.

They finished off their meal in short order after this, and, ten minutes later, were hurrying down the muddy streets to the place where the village tailed off into the woods and the mountain-path began. When they reached the mill-stream, now released from its winter bondage of ice, they found the old man there, with the lighted lanterns —four of them. He had taken the precaution to bring extra candles and some boxes of matches, and also a bundle of alpenstocks, which were carried by his housekeeper's nephew, Karl. These he distributed among the girls, reserving the two best for the ladies. Then, to the amazement of them all, he stooped down, swung small Laurenz Maico up on his shoulder, and announced his intention of escorting them to the school. 'I teach tomorrow,' he rumbled in his big deep voice. 'I may as well go up now. Herr Denny, he will give me a room in his chalet at Buchau, and I shall be of assistance to you *nicht wahr*?'

Miss Annersley accepted his offer with gratitude. She was not specially nervous, but the night was drawing on, and the path under the trees would be very dark when twilight had deepened into night. He nodded at her words of thanks, held out an arm for Jo, who was a prime favourite of his—perhaps the fact that she did not learn music from him had something to do with it—beckoned Frieda to join them, and strode to the head of the procession. He carried a lantern as well as Laurenz, and he marched on with the mountaineer's long slow stride that can be maintained for hours and which eats up the miles. The girls easily kept pace with him, and they found themselves getting farther and farther up the path, and nearer and nearer to school. He rumbled away to them about things in general as he went, and only paused once to move Laurenz so that she was more comfortable. Their lights swung along, making circles of yellow glow among the dark trunks of the trees, and their steps splashed through puddles and mud in fine style. Luckily, the rain held off, and they had reached the top of the path before they realised it almost.

'Only the lake-path now!' exclaimed Miss Annersley. 'Really we have done it extraordinarily well! The girls must go straight to bed when they have had something to eat, and then we shall be able to settle down to ordinary work tomorrow. I do hope this is the last excitement for this term!'

'There's the sale next Saturday,' Miss Stewart reminded her.

'I call that "ordinary" work,' replied Miss Annersley, laughing.

However, her hopes were in vain. They had reached the gate of the Chalet School before they felt the first drops of rain that heralded the coming of a deluge. Headed by Jo they raced up to the house like mad things, and burst in, to be immediately surrounded by an agitated crowd, who demanded with one voice, 'Have you seen anything of Eustacia?'

Chapter XXIII

'WHERE IS EUSTACIA?'

HERR ANSERL was the first to answer. Setting Laurenz down carefully, he shut the door behind them, since the rain was pouring in, and then turned to the excited mob of girls around them. 'Why do you ask that?' he rumbled. 'She was not with these. How, then, should we have seen her?'

'She is missing,' replied Deira. 'She hasn't been seen since last night. Violet and Greta didn't worry about her when they got up—they had a row with her last night. Then, when the bell rang for *Frühstück*, and she still didn't seem to be moving, they called to her, and then went into her cubicle. She wasn't there, so Vi ran to tell Mademoiselle. No one knows anything more about her than that, but the side-door was open when Luise came down this morning.'

At this point Mademoiselle appeared. 'Go back to your rooms, girls!' she said sharply. 'Why are you here? You know very well that you were told to stay in the common-room or your form-rooms!'

The crowd melted at once, and the newcomers were left.

Herr Anserl came forward. 'I am grieved to hear this, Mademoiselle,' he said. 'Pray, command me.'

Mademoiselle put up a hand and pushed her hair back from her face. 'I have no idea what to do,' she said wearily. 'We have rung them up at the Sonnalpe, and Dr. Mensch is coming down. He could not come before. The valley men have been out ever since *Mittagessen* looking for her, but so far we have had no news.' She turned to the startled girls, and spoke to them.—'Girls, can you think of any place where Eustacia can have gone? We have nothing to guide us—nothing to help us! I do not know what to do.— Joey, you know this place better than any other here. Can you make any suggestion?'

But Jo, with her black eyes widened till they looked

143

ready to drop out, could only shake her head. 'I haven't the least idea where she can be, Mademoiselle,' she said. 'Has she run away, or is it only a joke, do you think?'

'I fear she has run away,' sighed Mademoiselle. 'Oh, *mes enfants*, why did you not warn me that such a thing might happen? Why did you not say that she was so unhappy that she would do this mad thing? The poor child! And it has been raining in the mountains all day. The river is swollen already and floods the path. If we have such another flood as we had that first spring that we were hear, I fear for her very life.'

Miss Annersley put the girls gently to one side, and came and put an arm round her chief's shoulders. 'Mademoiselle, you are worn out,' she said quietly. 'You cannot think clearly at present. Come with me, and let me get you something to calm you. Miss Stewart will look after the girls. When you are calmer, we will go over all the clues we have, and see what we can make of them. Come!—Will you come to, Herr Anserl?'

Mademoiselle was really worn out, as Miss Annersley had said. She had wakened with a headache that morning, and, by this time, she was nearly blinded with pain. She allowed the senior-mistress to lead her into her little study, and submitted to being put into a big chair. Then, while Herr Anserl kept watch over her, Miss Annersley went for Matron, who came with her, carrying a glass of something. Mademoiselle drank it off at once, without inquiring what it was, and ten minutes later she was sleeping.

'A draught?' queried Herr Anserl in a stentorian whisper.

Matron nodded. 'I tried to get her to take it before, but it was impossible. She must have sleep, or she will be collapsing. Now, Herr Anserl, if you will help me, we will get her to her own room. She'll be safe enough for the next few hours.'

'Stand aside,' rumbled the shaggy musician, and he stooped and swung the unconscious woman into his arms.

Matron led the way to Mademoiselle's room, and he laid her on the bed, and then retired to join the girls and Miss Stewart. Joey, coming down from the dormitory whither she had been sent to change her stockings, saw him through the banister railings, and paused a moment. She was on the landing on to which the door of the Violet dormitory opened, and she opened it and went in. The dormitory looked much as usual. Someone had made Eustacia's bed in readiness, and every cubicle was as neat as always. Even on such an occasion as this, Matron had not relaxed her rules. Jo went into Eustacia's little domain, after she had switched on the light, and stood looking round. What she was expecting to see she herself would have been puzzled to say. She only knew that somewhere there was a clue. She opened the drawers of the bureau casually, but they were only filled with underclothes, neatly folded and arranged. She pulled down the bedclothes and examined the pillows, with memories of how she herself had left a message for her sister on that occasion when she had gone off after Elizaveta, Crown Princess of Belsornia, when her father's cousin had attempted to kidnap her. But the pillows had no note pinned to their snowy whiteness, and the bed showed nothing out of the way. With a dreary sigh, Jo drew up the sheets again and turned away. She glanced up at the curtains, which were always swung clear during the day that the cubicles might be as airy as possible. They had been dropped at night as usual, but Violet had swung them up that morning when she had made Eustacia's bed. Idly, Jo stretched up and pulled them down, swinging them along the bars that held them, so that the cubicle was shut off. Then she uttered a cry. Pinned to the one that hung between Eustacia and Greta was a tiny three-cornered note!

Jo snatched the pin out. Then, holding it folded as it was, she raced downstairs, shouting at the top of her voice, 'Mademoiselle—Matron! I've found a note!'

Matron demanded, 'What have you there?'

'A note pinned to one of her cubey curtains,' replied Jo. 'Where's Mademoiselle?'

'In bed and asleep,' replied Matron. 'You can't disturb her, Jo. Come with me to Miss Annersley.'

Jo followed Matron along to the staff-room, where the agitated staff were discussing matters and wondering what on earth they had best do next. At sight of the pair they started up.

'News?' asked Miss Annersley briefly.

'A note,' replied Matron with equal brevity.

Jo held it out.

Miss Annersley took it and tore it open. 'It's addressed to you, Joey!' she cried.

'Oh, never mind that!' pleaded Joey. 'Just read it, and see what she says!'

Miss Annersley read it through to herself. Then she turned to the others. 'Of all the extraordinary children!' she exclaimed. 'Listen to this!' Standing where the best light should fall on the minute writing, she read aloud: ' "Dear Josephine, I am running away, and I am going home. I refuse to stay here any longer. Your abominable treatment of me is too much. I have plenty of money with which to pay my fares, and I shall be quite safe. When I reach home I intend to write to the *Times,* exposing this School. I hope to ruin it.—Eustacia Benson." '

There was a short silence when Miss Annersley had finished. Characteristically, Jo was the first to speak. 'Coo! She must be dippy!' she exclaimed.

Matron said, 'Well, what are we going to do?'

'But which way did she go?' demanded Jo. 'We didn't meet her in Spärtz or Innsbruck; and anyhow, if they'd seen her at Spärtz, everyone knows our uniform, and someone would have stopped her, or said something to us when we got there.'

'That's true,' said Miss Stewart thoughtfully. 'Still, I suppose we had best ring them up at the station and ask if they have seen anything of her. And what about ringing up Herr Anserl's housekeeper and getting her to make inquiries in the town?'

'Yes,' replied Miss Annersley. 'We must do that first of all. But if she hasn't gone to Spärtz, where can she have gone?'

'D'you think she has taken the diligence to Germany?' asked Miss Wilson, who was there in her chair.

'There wouldn't be one at night, and there isn't one on Sundays,' replied omniscient Jo.

Miss Annersley got up from her seat. 'Then that's settled. If she didn't go by way of Spärtz and Innsbruck, she must have attempted to get into Germany over the Tiern Pass.'

'What—Eustacia?' gasped Joey. 'Why she simply hated walking!'

'In her present state of mind I don't suppose she would bother about that,' replied Miss Annersley. 'Poor child— poor, silly child!'

Jo looked outraged, but the senior-mistress said no more.

Miss Stewart explained. 'Think of her life, Joey! She was

146

brought up by two elderly people, who appear to have had some extraordinary ideas about education. They died, which was probably a greater shock to her than any of us, herself included, have realised. She was pitchforked—first into a family of jolly, ordinary boys; then into a girls' school, where she soon found that most of her old ideas were wrong. She is involved in nothing but trouble from the time she comes. I don't know what that library business of yours may have been, but obviously it hurt her pretty badly. She began to hate you, and because she knew that your sister was largely connected with the School, she is now trying to do the School an injury, hoping thus to make you feel some of the unhappiness she has felt.'

Jo looked as if her mind was in a perfect whirl—as, indeed, it was. Miss Annersley had vanished to ring up Spärtz; but when Miss Stewart stopped speaking, Miss Wilson took up the tale. 'There is one other thing—and if you were a different kind of girl, Jo, I shouldn't dream of mentioning it. As it is, I don't think it will affect you badly, though it may help you to be more thoughtful. Have you ever realised what a tremendous power you have in the School?'

'*Me?*' Joey sounded both flustered and embarrassed.

'Yes—you. No other girl has ever had so much influence. And it doesn't all—or even most—arise from the fact that you are Mrs. Russell's sister. It is your own self—your personality. You have had more to do with making the School what it is than almost anyone else—always excepting Madame. You have rarely come into contact with anyone who actively disliked you before, have you? Well, then, that is what was the matter. Eustacia felt your charm, even though she didn't understand what it was. She resented your treatment of her bitterly, and she tried to hate you for it. But it has been a hard battle, and, under all her assumed hatred, there has been a longing for your friendship. You have the most responsible gift of all, and I want you to realise it, and try to live up to it. Wherever you go, you are likely to find friends, and people will be anxious to win your liking. What you do and say will have a great influence on them. It has been so with Eustacia. In doing this mad thing, she is, unconsciously, trying to win your admiration. She is taking risks that ought to thrill you. I don't for one moment suppose that she knows all this; but

I know that that is what she feels. Now you may go, and please go straight to bed. Matron will bring you something to eat, and then you are to try to go to sleep. You are very tired, and you have had a good deal to consider. Tomorrow you will not go into school, and I want you to think over all this. Go now, dear. Good-night.'

'Good-night,' mumbled Joey; and left the room wondering if she were standing on her head or her heels.

'Do you think it was wise to say all that to her?' asked Miss Stewart.

'Yes; I think so,' said Miss Wilson gravely. 'Joey Bettany has a tremendous power in her hands, and she ought to be learning to use it rightly. She isn't a baby now, and she *is* a girl who thinks. I might have dreaded telling another type of girl all this; but it won't hurt Jo.'

In this she was quite right. Joey was not inclined to be uplifted by the thought that she possessed such influence over her fellow-creatures. Far from it, she almost resented it. Jo hated the idea of any responsibility, and if all 'Bill' said were true, then she had a tremendous responsibility, which she must carry through life. 'It's worse than being head girl!' she groaned to herself, as she shed her garments and got into her pyjamas. 'I shall be scared to speak in case anything I say may set someone doing mad things! Oh! How *rotten* it all is!'

She flounced down on to her knees to say her prayers, but, for once in her life, found it hard to repeat the words she generally murmured so glibly. Finally, she buried her head in her plumeau, and muttered rapidly, 'Please, God, if all that's true that Bill said, help me to play the game. And look after Eustacia. Amen.'

Then she got up, feeling a little easier, and when Matron came up with her tray, she was sitting up in bed, reading. 'Any news from Spärtz?' she asked, as Matron set the tray on her knees.

'Matey' shook her head. 'No one has seen her. I am afraid the silly child has really attempted the Pass.'

A gust of wind dashed the steadily-pouring rain against the window at that moment, and Jo shivered. 'Then she must be out in all that. How *awful*!'

'It is bad,' said Matron gravely.

Jo listened to it for a moment. Then her ear was caught by a new sound. With a sudden movement that almost overturned her tray, she jerked round. 'Matey! The river! It's in flood! Listen to it! It must be coming down like a mad thing! If—if Eustacia—gets caught——'

'I don't suppose for one moment that she will be,' said Matron calmly. 'Take your tray, Jo, and for mercy's sake don't upset it all over the bed! I have enough to see to without having to bother about fresh bed clothes for you!'

The matter-of-fact words calmed Jo considerably. She took her tray and sipped the hot milk that Matron had brought her. But when it came to the bread and butter, she found it impossible to eat.

Matron, watching her, refrained from forcing the food on her. She insisted on the milk being taken, and then removed the tray. 'Now, lie down again,' she said. 'I shall cover you up, and you must try to go to sleep.'

'But I can't!' said Jo. 'I can't go to sleep till I know that Eustacia is safe! Honestly, Matey, I can't!'

Matron pressed her down with a firm hand and covered her up. She had no intention of risking a bad night for Jo, who was already tired out. On principle, she rarely gave sedatives to the girls, but in this instance she felt it the only thing to do, and she knew that before half an hour was over Jo would be sleeping sweetly.

She was justified in her belief. When she slipped upstairs in her next spare moments, Joey was slumbering as soundly as a baby, and already the white tired look was fading from her face. Matron nodded her head triumphantly and returned to her duties again.

Meanwhile, where was Eustacia?

Chapter XXIV

EUSTACIA IS FOUND

WHERE was she, indeed? Up in a little cleft in the mountains, watching with terrified eyes the rising of the relentless grey waters that seemed to her to be getting nearer and nearer with every moment. With her face and hands brier-torn and bespattered with mud; her hair loose and wet and tangled by the wind; her clothes soaked through and clinging clammily to her, Eustacia would have been unrecognisable to anyone who had known her ordinarily. Her face was white with fear, and her eyes red with tears. Even as she crouched there, sobs shook her at intervals. Never in all her short life had she known such terror. And there was no help to be found anywhere. Again and again she had called, only to have her cries flung back by the mocking echoes, till she gave up calling in sheer desperation.

If only she could, by wishing, have found herself safely back in the Chalet School in the very thick of trouble, how ardently would she have wished it!

The rapid swirling past of the water was making her dizzy, and now a fresh horror came to join the others. Supposing she were to lose consciousness and roll down from her refuge into that hungry, cruel water! No one would know anything about it, and she would be unable to help herself. They would find her dead body some morning, and they would never know how it had happened.

At this point the poor child lost complete self-control and screamed till she was hoarse. It was only instinct that kept her clinging to the rock, in the niche of which she had taken refuge. Luckily, instinct saved her, and she clung there like a mad thing. Presently the terror subsided, and she fell into a state of semi-consciousness, in which she went over all that had happened since she had stolen out of the Chalet at six that morning to take the way over the great Tiern Pass into Germany.

It had seemed so easy at first. She had plenty of money, for her uncle had seen to it that she was not short of cash at school. She had guessed that she might be recognised in Spärtz as coming from the Chalet School, and she had no clothes with her but the regulation outfit.

Equally, she knew that there would be no diligence from Scholastika at the far end of the lake on Sunday. Her best scheme, therefore, was to go over the Pass on foot and get into Germany that way. From Germany it would surely be an easy matter to reach England, and then she would go home to Oxford and *stay* there. Of the necessity for passports and visas she never thought, if, indeed, she knew of it. It would be a hard journey, but regular walks and games had, to a certain extent, hardened her muscles, and she felt confident that she would be able to manage it.

She had heard the others talking of the mountain-stream that, for a certain distance, followed the road to the Pass, and she felt that if she went along the lake shores till she reached its outlet to the lake, and then took it as her guide till it turned to the mountains, she could not lose her way. And once she got that far she ought to be able to get across the Pass without losing herself. What she had not reckoned with was the rain, which, just as she had left the Briesau fence, came down like a silver mist, making it impossible to see more than a yard or so ahead. In addition, the stream was already swollen, and the water came across the path in places. Small wonder, then, that she missed the turn which should have taken her to the Pass and comparative safety, and finally she found herself lost on a rocky mountain-slope, with the thunder of the water in her ears and the mist of rain all about her.

Whatever faults she may have had, Eustacia Benson was not lacking in courage, and though she quickly realised that she had lost herself, she soon decided to turn back and get to the path again. Suddenly, above the raging of the waves, she heard a roaring that filled her with dread of she knew not what. It was not ordinary thunder—of that she was certain. Some queer instinct drove her away from the stream and up the mountain-slopes to the narrow cleft in which she now was; and even as she went there came into sight something that almost paralysed her. Tossing a crest of greyish foam, a wall of water swept down on her with awe-inspiring majesty and a noise that filled every corner. With a wild shriek, Eustacia clawed her way up to the cleft, and reached it just in time. Even as she scrambled up, the water passed over the spot on which she had been standing a moment since, and tore down to the valley. Other waves followed, but none so terrible as the first. Their action brought the stream very near her refuge, and she could get no higher.

If they had continued, she must have been swept away and drowned. Mercifully, the bulk of the water had come with the first two or three of the waves, and the rest was not sufficient to bring the river to her level. When Jo heard of it later, she said that a dam must have been formed up in the mountains by tree-trunks and underbrush being caught together. Under the increasing pressure of the water it must have burst suddenly, and the great waves were the result. It had happened before, and it would, no doubt, happen again. The unfortunate part was that Eustacia had seen it almost at its worst. By the time it reached the valley much of its force had been spent, and though they were flooded, it was nothing like so terrifying as it must have been up there in the mountains, confined in a narrow, rocky passage, which forced it to greater heights.

Unluckily for Eustacia, she knew nothing of this, and throughout that awful day she remained in her cleft, dreading the appearance of fresh walls of water and her own ultimate death by drowning. Then night came down, and though the rain had ceased during the afternoon, it returned at dusk, and poured down with a violence that beat the turbulent stream almost flat.

Eustacia crouched where she was and sobbed pitifully. As a matter of fact, she had less to fear from the water than before. The bulk of the flood had already gone past, and there was no further need to fear it. But of that she had no knowledge, and so she stayed, nearly crazy with fear and growing faint with hunger. By and by she sank into a kind of coma, and lay, unknowing of all that was passing, her fingers still digging into the crevices of the rock with a death-like grip which saved her from the results of any sudden movement.

And meanwhile the valley folk, once the worst of the flood had passed to the lake, were busily hunting for her. Men went along the Pass towards the German end, carrying lanterns and sticks, and calling lustily as they went, pausing every now and then to listen if there were any reply. Others followed the stream as far as was safe, employing the same means. One party even passed within calling distance of her refuge; but she was then unconscious and knew nothing of it.

At the Chalet School anxiety mounted higher and higher as the hours passed, and still no news came of her. Dr. Jem put in an appearance, soon after midnight, accompanied by Dr. Gottfried Mensch. The girls had all been sent to bed long since, and Miss Wilson had gone, too, at Matron's behest. The little ones, from whom, as far as possible, the worst had been kept, slept as usual, but many of the elder girls lay awake, listening and praying.

Gottfried Mensch knew the district thoroughly, and when he heard all Miss Annersley had to say, he nodded his head thoughtfully. 'If she has tried the Pass, and they have not found her, then there can be only two explanations of it,' he said. 'She must have slipped and fallen somewhere; or she followed the stream—as she would be likely to do, since you say she has not much knowledge of the route—and went too far. In that case, she is probably in some corner of the rocks, held there by the floods.'

Miss Annersley went white. The floods had washed up to the first-floor windows of the hotels and chalets built on the banks of the stream. If Eustacia had been caught . . . She dared not finish the thought, even to herself.

Gottfried saw it, however, and tried to reassure her. 'Believe me, Mademoiselle, it is most probable that she escaped to some niche in the rock. Then, the horror of it all may have caused her to faint, and when she came to, she found that she must stay where she was till the waters went down. It is a good thing that this stream sinks almost as rapidly as it rises. By dawn it will not be so very much higher than its banks, and it will be possible to follow it and examine the sides by daylight. I will take a lantern now, and go as far as I dare by its light, but I doubt if we shall find anything until the morning.'

He set off at once, and Dr Jem went to see Jo and Mademoiselle, who were both sleeping still. In Jo's room, Mary was awake, and when she heard him she called to him softly, 'Dr. Jem! Is that you? Oh, *have* they heard anything?'

He drew back the curtains that divided the little room, and came in and sat down on the edge of the bed. 'Nothing as yet, Mary. Gottfried Mensch says that he thinks she got caught in a cleft in the rocks by the flood, and has had to stay there till it went down. He is hunting now, and when daylight comes he will go up to the mountains with some of the men, and will seek till he finds her.'

Mary nodded tearfully. She choked back her sobs, for Matron had warned them that Jo must not be disturbed. Then she said, 'Do *you* think so, Dr. Jem?'

'I do,' said Jem solemnly. 'Now, Mary, lie down and go to sleep like a good girl. You can do nothing now, but if you are fresh and fit tomorrow, you may be able to help us very much. Good-night.'

Mary lay down and closed her eyes. 'Good-night,' she

said. And such was the force of his influence, she fell asleep very soon, and never stirred the rest of the night.

When the dawn came, Gottfried, with half a dozen trusty fellows from the valley, set off for the mountains. The rain had cleared off by this time, and a fierce west wind was driving the waters of the lake to madness. Already the flood was sinking, though it was still knee-deep in places, and they had to go carefully. When they reached the mountains it was better, for the water drained down into the bed of the stream, and in many places the old path was practically free again.

For three long hours they climbed, and then one of the men suddenly uttered a shout and pointed upwards to a niche in the rocks. 'She is there, Herr Doktor! *Das Mädchen* is there!'

Gottfried turned, and saw the little bundle of human misery that lay where the man was pointing. With three long strides he had reached the place and was bending over her. Eustacia lay very white and still, but not, as he first feared, dead. Her pulse beat feebly under his fingers, and she was breathing.

Rapidly he stripped off her soaking wet clothes and wrapped her in a rug he had strapped to his shoulders. Then he rubbed her temples and wrists and lips with brandy till the blueness left her and her breathing seemed deeper. Then, lifting her in his strong arms, he bore her downwards for a hundred yards. Arrived at a convenient place, he laid her down again, and proceeded to administer artificial respiration, until his own arms ached badly and the sweat stood on his brow. Then, satisfied that she was safe enough for the present, he resigned her to two of the men, who carried her carefully between them till they reached the valley. There Dr. Jem met them with a car. Over the squelching meadow-land they ploughed their way, till they reached the deep ditch that had been dug round the Chalet grounds to carry off the water of just such floods as this, and there they abandoned their car. They carried the senseless child across the playing-fields to the school, where she was taken to the sick-room and speedily tucked up in hot blankets.

In the study Madge Russell, who had come down that morning, faced her husband with eyes that held a great dread. As she noted the smile in his, the dread vanished, and she caught Mademoiselle in her arms, with a sound between a sob and a laugh. 'It is all right, Elise!' she cried. 'Jem is smiling! She is safe!'

Chapter XXV

'GOOD-BYE, EUSTACIA!'

YES, humanly speaking, she was safe. But her punishment was by no means over, and her worst enemy could not but have been sorry for her during the coming months. That wild scramble to safety had been achieved only at the cost of a sprained back-muscle, and the long hours of lying in a twisted and unnatural position had made matters worse. When Eustacia awoke from the long, deep sleep into which she had fallen just before Dr Jem came to tell the waiting women in the study that all should go well, it was to pain and helplessness such as she had never imagined before. For a fortnight the torture of every movement filled all her thoughts, and in her sufferings she forgot all about her awful experience on the mountain-side. Strangely enough, it never came back save as a vague dream might have done. Jem was thankful for this. He had feared the strain on her nerves. But Nature, kinder in some way than man, had ordained that fortnight's weary ache-ache-ache, and all but the dimmest remembrances had faded from Eustacia's mind on the day that she was first able to make any movement without pain.

By the end of a month they were able to prop her up slightly with pillows, but everything had to be done slowly. As Dr. Jem said, sprained and bruised muscles must always take their own time. Later would come massage and other treatment; but, for the present, Dame Nature must be allowed to manage in her own time.

'When may I get up, Doctor?' Eustacia asked him one day.

He looked down at her with a kindly smile. 'Well, not just yet, Eustacia.'

Eustacia sighed. 'I know that, thank you. I meant how long must I lie here?'

Her aunt, who had been sent for the day after that disastrous expedition of hers, and who was still with them, looked at the doctor with apprehension in her eyes. She laid a hand on Eustacia's, and Eustacia's thin fingers closed over it. During these weeks she had learnt to value her Aunt Margery's kindness very highly.

Dr. Jem sat down, and looked at her gravely. 'How plucky are you, Eustacia?' he asked.

'I—I don't know,' stammered Eustacia shrinkingly. 'Oh, Dr. Jem, it isn't going to be long, is it?'

'Longer than any of us like,' he replied. 'Now, listen to me, Eustacia. You have hurt the muscles of your back, and muscles are things that take some time to heal. If you want to get better as quickly as possible, you will do all I tell you, and do your best not to fret or complain. There is only one way at present in which you can be cured, and that is by absolute rest. You must not try to do much with your arms, even. You must never attempt to lift yourself. And, above all, you must be happy and cheery. Nerves and muscles are closely allied, you know, and the one reacts on the other. If you fret and grumble, and upset your nerves by crying, you will be months longer in winning a real cure. But if you do as I say, I see no reason why, by September, you may not be walking about; and by Christmas, unless you do anything silly, you should be quite all right again. You are to stay up here at the Sonnalpe till September at least, for the days will be very hot down at Briesau, and the cooler air up here will be better for you. Mrs. Russell and I and all the others will do everything we can to make the time pass more easily. Relays of the girls will be coming each week-end, so you need not feel yourself quite cut off from school. But, when all is said and done, there will be many times when things will seem horrid and dull and miserable. And those are the times when you've got to be brave and make up your mind to bear things as well as you can. Now, do you understand?'

'Yes,' said Eustacia. 'I do. I—I'll do my best, Dr. Jem.'

He took her hand in his and squeezed it gently. 'Good for you, Eustacia! And, by the way, isn't there any possible way of abbreviating that lengthy name of yours? If there isn't, we simply must find a nickname for you! Life's too short to go through the world shouting "Eustacia" every time we want you!'

'Mademoiselle called me "Stacie" the last time she came to see me,' said Eustacia, with a smile.

'Bravo, Mademoiselle! "Stacie" it shall be! And now, I must go. Keep your chin up, and don't let anything like a few months of lying more or less flat flatten your spirit. We can't help our bodies, but we *can* help our souls!'

And, with this sapient advice, Dr. Jem left the room and Eustacia was alone with her aunt. She was silent at first, for she was trying to take in all he had told her. Once, this would not have seemed so terrible, but a new Eustacia had been slowly growing during those unhappy weeks, and the new Eustacia wasn't sure that, even with her beloved books, she could altogether make light of her sentence.

Aunt Margery bent over her. 'Eustacia, you must remember what Dr. Russell said, and try not to fret, dearie,' she said. 'I must go home in another fortnight, for I'm sure my sons are getting into all sorts of mischief now that I'm not there to look after them. But we are all coming out for the summer holidays, and the doctor assures me that you will be in a wheel-chair by that time, and the boys will be able to wheel you all over. And Mrs. Russell will be with you as much as possible, and there will be Baby David to play with. It won't be all bad, little girl.'

Eustacia smiled up at her aunt. 'I know it won't, Auntie,' she said. 'I'm going to do my best to be brave as Dr. Jem said. After all, you know, the Robin has to give up all sorts of jolly things because she's not strong enough for them, and she never frets about it. If a babe like that can do it, then *I* can!'

There was one other thing Eustacia proved herself brave enough to do.

The Easter holidays were nearly over before Joey came up to the Sonnalpe, whither Eustacia had been carried at the earliest opportunity. Jo had been to Vienna, to spend a fortnight with Marie von Eschenau, and to stay for a week-end in Wanda's charming little flat. Three days before school began, she returned to the Tiern valley, and Jem brought her straight up to the Sonnalpe and Die Rosen, the Russell's home, where Eustacia had been established.

After a rapturous greeting from her sister and the Robin, and some time spent in playing with the twins and Baby

David, Joey got up from the floor. 'First, how is Eustacia?' she demanded.

'*Stacie* is getting on very well,' replied Madge, with a smile.

Jo's eyes widended. 'Mean to say she's let you abbreviate her name?' she said incredulously.

' "Eustacia" is too long for everyday work,' said Madge. '"Stacie" is far better.'

'I should say it *was*! What I meant, though, was that she must have changed a lot to allow anyone to cut off any of her syllables!'

'No,' said Madge, removing the end of the hearth-rug from her son's mouth. 'It was there all the time, only buried rather deeply. Now we've got all those layers scraped off, and we're finding that Stacie is underneath—not Eustacia at all. You can run along and see her if you like.'

Jo nodded and strolled out of the room, whistling. Madge looked after her with a smile. She was not deceived by Jo's nonchalance, and she knew that the young lady was feeling rather uncomfortable in reality.

Jo strolled on till she reached the door of the room which had been allotted to Eustacia. Here she tapped, after a moment.

'Come in!' called a cheerful voice. 'I'm all alone!' And Jo was very nearly stricken dumb with surprise. It was Eustacia's voice all right—but what a difference!

She pushed open the door and entered. There were differences in more than the tones of a voice. Jem had insisted that, so long as Eustacia was likely to be in bed, she must have her hair cropped, and it had been cut with a fringe so that there might be no slides to hurt her head. The change made by that alone was amazing. The hair was wavy, and the fringe made all the difference in the world, now that her high forehead was hidden. A faint pink in her cheeks spoke well for life on the Sonnalpe; and the smile with which she greeted the dumbfounded Jo was full of friendliness. 'Joey!' she said. And that, in itself, was a shock, for before, Eustacia had always insisted on giving Jo her full name.

Joey came and sat down on the chair by the bedside. 'Hullo!' she said awkwardly. 'Feeling fitter today?'

'Lots,' said Eustacia firmly. Her eyes met Joey's. There was a moment's constraint. Then, suddenly, both girls burst

158

out laughing. That happy shared laugh cleared the air, and when they were grave again, it was not hard for Eustacia to do what she had made up her mind to do. 'Joey,' she said, 'I want to say I'm sorry for being such a beast to you last term. It—it was my fault there's been so much trouble about the Robin——'

But Joey wouldn't let her go on. 'The Robin's much better again,' she said. 'And I was almost as much to blame as you. I'm a tactless ass—as people frequently tell me—and I put your back up. I'm sorry too, Eustacia. There's no sense, though, in us both going on apologising to each other, is there? Let's take it as read and begin again.'

Eustacia put out her hand. 'Shake,' she said tersely, remembering a favourite expression of her cousin Ned's.

Jo took it and shook it very gingerly. 'An' now,' she said, 'I'm going to call you "Stacie" like the others. I'll rub it well into the School, and when you come back in September, no one will remember anything at all about Eustacia. So that's settled. Now, tell me! Have you seen Gisela's baby yet?—and what she's like?'

'Madame brought her yesterday for ten minutes,' said Eustacia, 'and she's sweet. They are going to call her "Natalie", after Dr. Mensch's little aunt who died so long ago.'

'Good!' said Jo. 'That's sweet of Gisela. I do wish *die Grossmutter* had lived long enough to know of that.'

'Herr Mensch is awfully pleased,' said Eustacia. 'He and Frau Mensch are still here, you know. And Frieda is, too.'

'Good old Frieda!' said Jo. Then she heaved a sigh. 'Oh, *aren't* we all growing up! Here's three of us married, and one a proud mamma, and I've got to be head-girl this coming term, and the Robin is going into the Second after the summer holidays. You stay a kid as long as you can, Stacie! Growing up's horrid!'

'It has its compensations,' said Madge's voice at the door. 'Now say good-bye to Stacie, Jo, and then you can run over to Gisela's and see her and the baby for a few minutes.'

Jo got to her feet. 'Back soon,' she said. 'Jolly glad to see you *at last*, Stacie. Your sister wasn't nice at all; but I'm jolly sure you're going to be one of us in no time!'

And a happy light was in Stacie's eyes as she replied, 'Good-bye, Jo. Eustacia wasn't nice, as you say. But I know Stacie will do her best to be a real Chalet School girl now and always.'